WOUNDING

WOUNDING

Heidi James

Bluemoose

First published in 2014 by
Bluemoose Books Ltd
25 Sackville Street
Hebden Bridge
West Yorkshire
HX7 7DJ

www.bluemoosebooks.com

British Library Cataloguing-in-Publication data
A catalogue record for this book is available from the British Library

Paperback ISBN 978-0-9927919-1-9

Hardback ISBN 978-0-9927919-0-2

Printed and bound in the UK by Short Run Press

Cover image: Maternal Affection by Edward Hodges Baily
in Victoria and Albert Museum

Cover photo by Tara Darby

There is no gratitude in mercy and in medicine.

Gertrude Stein, *Tender Buttons*

This book is dedicated to all mothers, everywhere.

Pristine, she is motionless as a length of white bandage is wound around her body. Hands lift her, turning her one way then the other. She is held tight by the soft bindings. Her eyes are covered, for they too were damaged. If she tries to open them she can just make out the light oozing through the weave of the fabric; she prefers to keep them closed. She is being cared for, nursed by an unseen strength that can lift her entire body easily. The bandage is wound around her arms, first separately, each one carefully covered from shoulder to fingertip; then they are bound to her body. She is as secure as a swaddled baby. Unable to move, unable to hurt herself, she is wrapped up against injury.

Every day they come in and unwind her, unveiling her new healing perfection. She is inspected; gentle fingers interrogate her flesh, probing the processes of her body. She is entirely clean. They bathe her with a warm fluid that doesn't cut like water but soothes and slides over her like oil. She is too precious and sensitive for water. She is massaged and preserved, turned regularly on her bed to protect her against pressure sores. She is undemanding, as malleable as modelling clay; she lets them move her here and there. They recreate her each time they touch her; she is remade. A tube through her nose delivers nutrients to her stomach; waste products are removed just as efficiently.

She is as contented as a stone. Moved by the will of others, she will go no further than this existence. She makes no decisions. Complete as she is, there are none to make. She is almost the same substance as the bed, as the floor, as the light fitting: she is inanimate; only the slight movement of her breathing differentiates her, but as it is involuntary and temporary it doesn't count for much.

She is reduced to a thing that loves. She loves the hands that cleanse and wrap her. She loves the white bandages. She loves the gurgle of the nutrients as they dribble through the tube into her. She loves the press of the entire universe on her unmoving body and the dreadful pull of gravity. She loves her transformation. She loves.

Cora steps down from the train. It's a long drop between the train and the platform, but she doesn't stumble. She yields to the flow of other bodies pushing her towards the exit and the ticket barriers with the usual staff leaning against the wall. She presses her card against the reader and the gates open for her, like blunt scissors. Outside it's still hot and light, despite being early evening. Taxis queue around the corner, waiting for the tired, the lazy and the lost. She walks past them, the slamming doors and the destinations, the meters set to clock the distance, the rolled up tabloids on the dashboard, the shiny shoes and loosened ties of office workers.

On the corner a man sits on the kerb, perilously close to the traffic, his grey beard growing towards his belly. He would look like Santa Claus if he scrubbed up and wore a red suit. He nods slowly back and forth, a can in his dirty hand, as if he's dancing to a song only he can hear. Something about the way he is sitting suggests he is younger than he looks. Cora thinks about speaking to him and checking if he's OK, perhaps suggesting he move, but then the moment has passed and she's walked by and she would have to turn back and probably bump into people walking behind her. He'll be fine, she thinks. Maybe the police will come by and sort him out for the night. She has things that she must do; she must focus.

She walks on through the streets, past the safe snug houses in their smug postcode. Past the dry gardens withering from the hosepipe ban, the cars cooling on concrete drives, their engines ticking like irregular clocks. She walks home slowly, her head dipping with each step, like a bird. She adjusts her black leather bag, heavy with her laptop and files, moving it to her shoulder. She looks straight ahead. She pays no attention to the cars flashing past, the glossy four-wheel drives ferrying children to ballet or flute classes, the plumber's van with its windows wound down and the radio loud enough for the whole street to hear, or the low black crawl of a vacant funeral limousine. She ignores the indifferent drift of other people: mothers pushing buggies; a cat crouched on a wall, flicking its white-tipped tail at the air; an old woman watering her hanging baskets from a glass jug; children swinging back and forth in the small park, behind the protection of iron railings. She is unaware of the green shape of her dress, folding and refolding around her knees as she moves forwards, a fluid progress through the atmosphere.

She is repeating her list of tasks for the rest of the day like a mantra. The tasks tether her, hold her firm. She knows that without them she would lose form and fade away, so she runs over them in her mind, turning them as if each task was a plump bead on an abacus, something she could feel, something to worry back and forth across a wire frame. The thoughts expand and the to-and-fro, the click and clack of the tasks becomes the rhythm of her steps. She has to stay focused on being who she is, who she must be.

Her hands, loose at her sides, feel nothing; the hot sun exerts no pressure on her bare head; her eyes are unsquinting in the brightness. Her mind feels granular, separated, the insulation of her body intervening between it and the outside world. Cora turns a corner into a street lined with narrow Edwardian houses. She takes a deep breath and stops outside a tall, red brick house. Her heart kicks like a rabbit against her ribs: she is here.

The routine will begin behind the blue solidity of the front door. She stands at the metal gate. Red and white striped curtains frame the bay window at the front of the house. She doesn't remember buying them, or even choosing them. Did she? Choose them? They seem brighter, more gaudy, today. She can't imagine standing in front of the fabric in a busy shop, feeling it, weighing it between her fingers, purchasing it. Who could have run them up on the sewing machine, measured the window, and hung them? All those actions feel alien to her, alien beyond comprehension. She stands there on the pavement looking at the stunted magnolia tree in the front garden, the street extending either side of her, the twin row of houses, inside which her neighbours are eating, pacing, sleeping, breathing, fucking, talking. Out of sight, out of mind. Concealing secrets like Russian stacking dolls, one after another, fitting neatly inside themselves, secret after secret swallowing each other whole.

She reaches into her bag and grabs her keys, cool to the touch. A bundle of keys, ten or so, different sizes: a small collection. She has keys for her parents' house, for work, for her old flat, for the car, for her jewellery box and, of course, for this house. She tries one, inserting it into the secret mechanism of the lock. The key opens the door. When she enters she will become another version of herself.

Once, when she was around twelve years old, she had come home from school to find no one there, the door locked. She tried the side gate and the garage, rattling at the padlocks, but they were shut firm too. The familiar house, with its spotless net curtains at the windows and neat, weed-free lawn had become strange, fastened shut against her. Like a friendly face refusing to smile.

Her mother was always home with her quiet busyness, bringing Cora juice and biscuits as she watched Blue Peter, her schoolbag dumped at the foot of the stairs, school shoes kicked off, white-socked feet tucked up on the sofa. Her mother was always there, lurking: busy, cleaning or cooking, breathless from climbing the stairs with clean laundry or pushing the vacuum cleaner around. But this one day she wasn't. Cora sat on the front step of the house, exhilarated by the idea of its emptiness. She was surprised by the thrill of being so close to peril. Waiting, while danger lurked out there in the town, on her own street even. She'd been warned about strangers who lured little girls away with sweeties and puppies and then never took them back home to their parents. She knew that anything could happen. Anything. But she wasn't afraid.

When her father came home from work at 5:15pm and saw her sitting there alone on the front door step, his face tightened, the weight of his anger pressing down on his brow, his jaw working as if he were chewing his own teeth. She knew that look: it was a look he seemed to keep especially for her mother. He climbed out of his car and she watched it rise up like a levitating body, the coiled suspension relieved of his weight. He slammed the door and the car rocked a little.

'Where's your mother?' he asked, his briefcase in one hand, the other hand reaching into his jacket for his house key.

'I don't know, Daddy.' Cora stood up and sucked in her bottom lip, scraping her top teeth against its soft flesh.

Just as he opened the door her mother arrived, flustered, panicked, her hair newly done, 'Sorry, so sorry, the perm took so long, I tried to hurry them along.' Her mother's hands flapped like washing pegged out in the wind, her voice disembodied, the words more vague impression than spoken statement. Cora's father sent her upstairs. 'I need to talk to your mother. Go to your room.'

She went to her room, to its pink and white walls, its flounces and frills, and sat on the bed, turning the pages of a book, while her father shouted at her mother for her stupidity and the neglect of his little girl. But Cora hadn't felt neglected. She'd felt liberated, completely loosened from the tight bonds of the family. Free for the first time she could remember, she could almost imagine she was an orphan. Rootless, she'd felt nothing but joy.

There are men working over the road, digging up the path. Most likely laying cables and such for all the new TV channels, phone lines and the Internet. All those words wriggling underground. Spooky idea. All that information on the move, hidden underfoot as you go about your business. Clueless as to what's being said, to what's known about us. Paranoid, you'd say. Maybe I am.

They've started early, hammering at the paving and tarmac. They'll wake you and the kids. I lie here listening, with you sleeping by my side. My hands crossed on top of the duvet, head propped up on pillows. The early light edging in under the blinds. It's not unpleasant. They occasionally shout to one another, over the sound of the drill. Laughing. Bit early for it, being a weekend; but you haven't stirred, you're lying on your side, curled up on yourself, your small hands tucked under your chin, your wedding ring just visible. You have no make-up on and look like a young girl, almost a child, not a woman, or a mother.

The banter from outside reminds me of when I was a student and did some labouring to earn enough to buy my first car. Dad didn't approve, of course. That was a fun summer, working on a building site, stripped to the waist, tanned and toned – I don't think I've ever looked so good. The money was great, too, for a seventeen-year-old. God, I loved that car. A VW Golf. Black and shiny, super quick, not flash, but not a rust bucket either. Bought all by myself with no help from the parents. That was a great time. University, mates, girls, a car. It's a cliché, but I was lucky. Had good friends from school who came down to Uni with me, our old gang all in Halls together. I liked going to the lectures, joined the rugby team, enjoyed the cheap beer, worked abroad in the summer and partied hard so I could focus on my studies in the term. Loved meeting new people, the sense of excitement, knowing that this was it, my life had really begun. I was even – and it's a little uncomfortable to think about now that we're married and have a daughter – a bit of a Jack-the-lad. Sleeping around, taking random girls back to my room. I thought I was quite the lover-man, Mr. Smooth. It wasn't anything outrageous: sowing my wild oats, that's all. I wonder what they're up to now, those girls, if they remember me. Probably married with kids, like the rest of us. I doubt I'd recognise them if I saw them again, nor they me. Good times though, good times.

I only had one really serious girlfriend before you. My mother said she was my first love, but she wasn't. You are. She was adorable and sweet, with short blonde hair. Lucy. Just Lucy, no nicknames or diminutives: she was very particular about her name. She was pretty particular about most things actually. She liked things to be just so. Not like you. I love that about you. That you don't sweat the details of life, you don't sulk if I haven't put my socks in the laundry basket, or I forget to put the bin out. I love you for more than that of course. You're the only woman I've ever truly loved and I know that will be so for the rest of my life. What we have is something completely different; you know I've never even looked at another woman since we've been together. Not seriously, at least.

It's funny, my mother loved Lucy more than I did. They played tennis together and lunched and planned and all the while I knew something between me and Lucy wasn't quite right. I mean, I was serious about her, I cared about her and she was the first woman I lived with and bought furniture with. I sent her flowers and nursed her through hangovers, colds and down days. I played golf with her dad and got on fine with her mother but, I don't know, it just didn't quite fit. It's a strange one that, knowing something isn't right, but you can't quite pin down exactly what it is. You like each other, you might even love each other, you even make each other laugh, but somehow you know that you don't really want to spend the rest of your life with this person, that marrying them could be a disaster. That there is someone out there better suited to you. I was working at Gilson's then, as you know of course, doing well, having been promoted to Senior Finance Manager, having good holidays, skiing in winter, at the beach in summer.

I'd bought a flat and a new car, all the stuff that you do because it's what you do and it's reassuring, knowing your role, having a plan and living up to expectations. I'd have married Lucy eventually, I suppose. Perhaps we would've made it work somehow, had kids and muddled through. Who knows? Who cares?

And then you came to work with us. And, me being me, I kept my head down and watched and fell in love and did nothing because I was committed to Lucy and as you've said, my darling, I'm a wimp, wanting to do the right thing all the time. So I was good, playing dutiful boyfriend, picking up after myself, cooking suppers, going shopping, visiting her parents on Sundays for lunch, pissing with the seat up, rinsing the sink out after brushing my teeth. I did the list of jobs Lucy wrote out for me every weekend and took her for dinner on a Saturday night. I was dutiful, but not attentive. All I could think about was you.

I can see you now, in your pencil skirts and high heels. You were so glamorous, smoking and drinking wine in the pub after work, holding your cigarette just like a film star of old, as if it were an accessory, some piece of jewellery created to accentuate your best features. And I was your work colleague, nothing more, watching you from afar, fascinated by even the simplest things you said or did. Like the way you lifted your hair from the back of your neck and twisted it up out of the way when you were concentrating or the way you'd let one of your shoes slip off your foot and dangle from your toe as you were talking on the phone. The irony, of course, is that while I was secretly, guiltily in love with you, Lucy was screwing some bloke she met at my mother's tennis club, and even though I was relieved not to be the one to end it, relieved not to be the bad guy, to be honest I was humiliated and hurt. No one likes to be rejected, do they? But I was free to ask you out. And I did. In the pub, during the regular Friday after-work drinks, I bought you a glass of wine and you looked straight at me. You looked right at me in a way that meant you saw me as I've never been seen before. I know that sounds stupid, but it's the only way I can describe it. You saw me.

Inside, behind the blue door, is the suck and fuss of her family, two little children and a husband. A house. A family. So much to get wrong, choices made that could lead to regret or worse, much worse. So far, so good. A decent education, some travel with friends that widened her horizons, a nice man, a boy and a girl child, a house with a garden, a career, motherhood. All the right choices; nothing had gone wrong. Nothing serious. No illicit love affairs, no unplanned pregnancies, no bankruptcy or addictions, no sudden tragedies: all present and correct.

She hangs her bag on the banister at the bottom of the stairs. The children are in the sitting room watching TV. She turns her palms inwards to hide a sudden sweat before wiping her hands on her dress. Down the hall in the kitchen, her husband stands by the sink, peeling potatoes. His patient hands feel the flesh of the vegetable for bruising or flaws before carefully peeling back the skin, rinsing the mud away under the cold tap as he works. A bristle of irritation catches the back of her throat: his hunched shoulders, untidy in his checked shirt, half-tucked into jeans she dislikes, straight dark hair on the nape of his neck. He looks up and sees her, his wife, her brown hair loose around her shoulders, her skin pale despite the sunshine.

'Hello darling. How was your day? How was the office?' Smiling, he comes forwards and kisses her, wiping his hands on a towel. He turns and reaches past her to the kitchen counter; everything well thought out, pre-planned, carefully administered.

'Here, I poured you some wine. Kids! Mummy's home!'

She takes the wine; the red liquid glows in the swell of the glass. She knows he doesn't like her to drink, but equally he doesn't like to seem oppressive. So he offers a civilised glass of wine with dinner, as is ordinary and perfectly acceptable to the rest of the world and which does not in any way indicate an alcohol problem. She sips carefully from the glass, slowly, demonstrating that she is firmly in control of her appetites.

'Thanks. I'm fine. Nothing out of the ordinary. You?'

The children rush in, their dark heads shiny, hair smoothed flat as if wet, just like him, their little bodies, only six and four years old, flexing and soft, never still, they wind themselves around their mother. She looks into the flat gape of their upturned faces, recognising him, his eyelashes, the compact ball of his nose, his thin lips: his children. She cannot see herself, yet they are hers. She knows they are: how can she forget the bloody processes that delivered them? Her blood thins, she thins, becomes less distinct, a silence erasing her, the hand that holds the glass, that pats the bodies of the children, is erased, removed from her mind, a mind swathed in a silence. She feels sick.

'I picked the kids up early so thought I'd get dinner on. I'm making cottage pie, OK?' He looks at her, his eyes wide and damp as if wanting to be petted for performing such a difficult task, wanting her approval like a large dog.

'Yes, sounds lovely.' The children continue their eel-like squirming around her feet. 'Have the kids eaten?' She forces herself to look him in the eye and smiles. He nods, efficient as always.

'I gave them beans on toast for supper.'

'I'll put them to bed, shall I?'

'Alright, Cora. Why not? They'd like that. Wouldn't you, kids?' He stretches his hand to her and hooks his little finger around hers, his thumb stroking her palm, tracing the life line, head line, her life supposedly mapped in the space of her hand. Standing, connected to him like that, she counts a polite beat of two before loosening herself from the children and stepping back, her husband's hand falling to his side. Looking at them—a matching trio framed by the duck-egg blue walls of the kitchen, the pale oak cupboards, ceramic sink, dark slate-tiled floor, childish splodges of poster paint on rough sugar paper taped to the fridge—they merge together with their environment. Belonging here and to each other.

'Right. Come on then. Let's get you ready.'

The children groan, 'I don't want to go to bed, Mummy. Daddy! Please let us stay up. Please!'

Cora turns and walks away, moving through the hall and up the stairs as if moving not through space but with space, as if behind her she trails a void, a vast blank nothing. The two children follow, giving up their protests. In the bathroom she squeezes toothpaste onto their brushes for them. The children silently work at their teeth, up and down strokes, up and down, the repetition of movements delaying the inevitable decay. She watches them, supervising the task as she is required to do, her arms crossed over her chest. She breathes slowly, in and out. Stay calm, staying calm. Breathe. She must at the very least keep watch over them, it shouldn't be too much to ask. The deep pile of the bathroom rug cushioning her feet, the children buried to their ankles in twisted wool. The back and forth of the plastic rod in their fresh mouths, delicate skin stretched over sharp little milk teeth... teeth that gnaw rather than tear or rip, like rodents rather than something carnivorous. They aren't dangerous. When they finish she automatically rinses the spat froth from the sink, wiping with her hand. Cleaning away every last trace. 'Go to your room, Patrick, and put your pyjamas on. I'll be through in a minute to tuck you in.' She takes the four-year-old girl by the hand and leads her through to her room. The little girl follows, looking up at her mother, her small tired eyes lingering on her mother's face but Cora doesn't look down, only looks ahead to the next task, and the next, and the next. Click clack click. She strips the child's clothes carefully, trying not to pull her long dark hair as she removes her t-shirt or catch her nails on the smooth flesh of the child's stomach. She is utterly careful, full of care and lacking love. Pulling off the girl's underwear, the naked little girl, unsexed, pristine, stands in front of her, her sturdy little legs pressed together. 'I don't want nappy. I want to go bed with no nappy.'

'Don't be silly, Jessica. You know you can't. You aren't clean at night yet. You have to wear a nappy.' She pulls one from a drawer under the child's small bed.

'Millie doesn't wear nappies ever.'

'Yes, well then Millie is a clever girl isn't she?'

'Only babies wear nappies.'

'Yes, I know, only babies wear nappies.'

'I'm not a baby.'

'Aren't you? Why behave like one then?' Cora tugs a clean nightgown over her daughter's head, covering the still-perfect female body, and placing her hand on the unguarded space between the girl's shoulder blades pushes her – gently – towards her child-sized white bed with its consolation of soft peach-coloured quilt and pillows. 'Time to sleep now, Jessica.' She smoothes the sheets, pulling back the covers, plumping pillows, her actions complete in themselves, unthinking. Instinctive, animal. The child climbs into her bed on top of the just-smoothed sheets, wrinkling them, pushing her small feet into the warmth of the feathered bed, a grubby toy rabbit clamped under her arm. 'Read me a story, Mummy. Please?'

Cora stands, her knees clicking, a sound as large as the small room, clicking like a doll's plastic limbs. 'Not tonight, Jessica. It's too late.'

'But Daddy...'

'It's too late, Jessica.'

'Daddy always reads me a story.'

'Well, I said no. Go to sleep.'

The child begins to whine, a strange non-cry that reminds Cora of the noises a nest of new kittens would make, still blind and fumbling, mewling incessantly. Cora folds her hands behind her back, and a bleak pulse seems to urge her – to reach out and pinch the flesh of the child's arm, or press her hand against its mouth and shut off the sound or to slap, and scratch and stop it, stop it in its plaintive individuality, its thoughts and words. Its endless needs. But she doesn't. She turns to leave the room.

'Don't turn off the light, Mummy.'

'There's nothing to be afraid of.' She switches off the light and pulls the door shut behind her.

The boy, her son, untouchable in his maleness, his mystery, recognisable but always unreachable, has changed into his Thomas the Tank Engine pyjamas.

'Hello, Mum.'

'Hello, Patch. Ready for bed?'

'S'pose, Can I have a story?'

'No, it's late.' She moves towards him. 'Get into bed, please.'

'I'm going to say my prayers first.' The boy kneels, the soles of his feet soft in the lamplight.

'I beg your pardon? What do you mean? Say your prayers! Who taught you to do that? I've never heard you say prayers before. Patrick, who taught you this?'

She reaches into the blue confines of his bed and begins smoothing the sheets. This repetition, a constant repetition of actions, her body a thought that thinks itself, frightens her, her mind not necessary to her body's maternal endeavours; her throat constricts as if compressed by hands.

'Miss Ingrams at school taught us. She said God listens to everything we say. She smells nice and she gives me a sweetie when I read to her.'

Cora is dead, a zombie, fleshy and visible, but constructed only of thoughtless, repetitive actions. Of angers and impulses, old gestures. The small boy kneeling next to her presses his hands together, his bitten nails ugly against his flesh.

'Dear God, please bless all the animals, and Daddy, and Jessica, and Mummy, and Grandma and Grandad, and all my friends and Miss Ingrams. Amen.'

'Don't pray, Patrick. It's silly, there is no one to hear you, trust me. Miss Ingrams is wrong. Completely wrong.'

'You're here, Mummy, and I can hear myself and God can hear me, Miss Ingrams said so.' His eyes unblinking, like a reptile.

'Yes, I'm here, but there is no God to listen to prayers. You understand? It's important you understand there is no God to help you or bless us all. It's a silly nonsense. You know that, don't you? It's a lie, like fairies and ghosts and goblins. Just a story.'

The boy shrugs. He will forget about saying his prayers in just a few days, they're just a newly acquired fad that will go the way of others, like skateboarding and collecting football game-cards. He slides into his bed. She presses her cheek against his, against the head that forced its way out of her, the head that thinks for itself, the head that contains thoughts of a benevolent god and she wonders just what he sees when he looks at her, and who she is in his thoughts. When will he learn to see her clearly? He will hate her. She can't bear to kiss him.

'Goodnight, Patch. Sleep tight.'

She leaves the room, walks down the stairs, each step repeating, the repetition, the stairs, her feet, her steps; and digs her nails deep into the flesh of her wrist, semi-circles of discomfort pulling her back into the solidity of her body.

I'm watching you sleep. I know every inch of your body and face but you're completely mysterious, lost in dreams. Your hair curls over the pillow. You're breathing slowly, quietly, your lips soft and slightly open. I wish I could say this to you now. Wish I could find a way to bring you back to me.

I came to pick you up from the flat you shared with Sandra. The flat was over a Chinese takeaway and the smell of cooking fat and chow mein was overpowering as I climbed up the narrow stairs to your door. Sandra let me in and I sat waiting for you in the small sitting room while she nattered about how lucky she was to have found such a great flat mate from an ad she'd placed in the paper. I was surprised by that, I imagined you lived with an old friend from Uni or school, not a stranger you'd met via a free ad. Seemed like a lonely thing to do, a loser's thing to do, if I'm honest. I remember thinking, 'Who does that? Who lives with nutters they know nothing about?' I wondered if you were a psycho with no mates. What a tool I was. But I've learnt a lot from you, most especially just how differently we all live our lives. I'd always been confident that there was one way to live and it was our way, the way my family did things. I just couldn't imagine anything else. All my friends, our circle, were the same too. There was school, holidays and university, learning to drive and a gap year, work and buying a house, all those things.

Walks in the country on a Sunday, tennis in the summer, a close circle of friends that connect you back to your family and then comes marriage, children, success. We all had the same expectations, I suppose, and things worked out the way we'd thought they would, bar the odd glitch here and there. But you were from somewhere different: you were exotic, with a different way of life. You seemed free, rootless.

I scanned the room looking for traces of you, something that would give me a clue – CDs or books, paintings, anything. I soon realised you had nothing to do with the cheap sofa, or the huge TV, or the Take That poster or the pile of celebrity gossip magazines on the coffee table. But at the time, I sat there in my too-tight new shoes, still clutching my jacket in nervous hands, wondering if I'd totally misjudged you. Perhaps you weren't so mysterious and sexy; perhaps you were the type of girl my mother and sister had taught me to despise. Frivolous and empty headed and a psycho to boot... Rightly or wrongly. Wrongly, it turned out because Sandra was a good friend and has been a good friend to both of us. See, I needed you to bring out the best in me.

Anyway, she chattered on about her job, the TV blared away, my shoes pinched and then you finally came in. Looking so completely different to the way you looked at work that I felt almost embarrassed: embarrassed that I'd intruded on an intimate moment, almost as if I'd walked in on you changing or something; or maybe it was just simple shyness. But it was like you were another person. An even more beautiful person, I hasten to add. You were wearing jeans, with a t-shirt and jacket. Hardly any make-up and your hair was still damp. You looked softer; you looked like you of course, but a different version. This was our first meeting outside of work with its suits and ties and expense accounts. If I'm honest, I was even more crazy about you. Sandra carried on chattering as we stood there looking at each other, all shy.

We walked to a little French restaurant just around the corner from your place. Past the dark Common and the pretentious little bistros all painted beige and gold with elaborate wine glasses, past the pubs and the fast food joints and the cinema. All the while I tried to think of what to say, how to dazzle you with my style and panache. You were quiet, but smiling, watching. Not shy or rude, you seemed happy not to have to fill the space with your voice. It was the sexiest thing I'd ever experienced, this quiet confidence. You watched and you listened. It gave me a hard-on. I wanted you. God, I wanted you so badly. So we went into this little old place with its gingham tablecloths and squat wine glasses and authentically rude waiters. I did my best to impress you with my schoolboy French. You didn't seem to notice. You looked around and smiled and listened. You tucked your hair behind your ear as you ate your scallop starter, revealing a thin gold hoop. I wanted to kiss you where it touched your neck. I didn't of course. You ate your steak and I messed around with a fish thing, unable to eat I was so entranced. I pushed it around and around my plate, in a way that would've infuriated my mother. I told you about my school and my parents and my sister. I told you about Uni and travelling to India and Australia. I wanted you to know everything about me. I wanted you to want me as much as I wanted you.

You ordered vanilla ice cream and an espresso coffee, and then you asked for an amaretto with two ice-cubes and a twist of lemon. So precise and efficient. I loved it. I wondered why you were so specific about the ice cubes, but didn't dare ask in case I looked like a gauche idiot. Stupid, the little things that one remembers, that one falls for. I asked for a Latte. The ice cream and coffees arrived and I watched as you poured the espresso over the dollop of yellow melting sludge and began to scoop up the slowly combining mixture. I'd never met anyone like you. All the girls I'd ever known fitted into a pattern, a mould. They did just what was expected of them. Just like all the blokes I've known I suppose. But you were different somehow, more immediate and present. And then you took a swallow of your amaretto and sucked in an ice cube. It sat on your tongue and you left it there whilst you listened to me drone on about work and numbers and the latest projections because I couldn't think of anything else to say and behind the flesh of your cheeks I could see the workings of your tongue and jaw as you massaged the ice cube around your mouth. It was so completely sexy, and odd at the same time. I wondered whether my mother would like you.

I asked you if you played tennis and you laughed out loud, not quite tipping your head back and howling with laughter, but almost. It seemed such an innocent question at the time.

You shook your head. Golf? More laughter. Skiing? Even more laughter. You took out your cigarettes and asked if I minded. I did of course, but I wasn't about to say so. I tried to be smooth and reached to light it for you, but you laughed again and moved back in your seat out of reach. You lit it yourself of course. Then blew out long streams of smoke that clouded around us both. I inhaled it, thinking to myself that this smoke had been inside your body. It was part of you. None of this I would've dreamt of telling you before. But I want to find a way to reach you. And the truth seems to be the only reliable thing. My mother always said one will avoid trouble with the truth. Would you listen if I woke you?

I walked you home. I still hadn't touched you, not even a brush of fingers. My whole body vibrated with the intensity of being near you. I felt like we weren't just two individuals walking along, but like some kind of energy connected us, that we were set apart from everyone and everything around us. I asked you where you grew up and went to school. You looked up at me and said 'Nowhere special' like that was enough of an answer. And you just stood there, looking up at me. My fingers played with the weight of my keys, wondering if now was the time to kiss you. Like comedy, timing is everything for the first kiss. I didn't want to mess it up. I wanted to impress you, to impress myself on you. A car crawled past us, its music blaring out. I let it pass. You cleared your throat and looked down at your feet. I stepped forwards, took my hands from my pockets and put them around your waist; I pulled you towards me. You were perfect. You tipped up your face and waited as I bent to your lips.

Cora sits at her desk, typing a report. Rows of hygienic numbers, infallible, logical and neat, pulse imperceptibly on her screen. She leans forward, her eyes narrowed, frowning. She types quickly, completely in control. The office is modern and new, with that chemical smell of plastic furniture and air conditioning. A wall of windows to her right reveals the Thames and Southwark beyond. She can see the tops of smaller, older buildings and the spires of churches. Below, people flow along the tributaries of the streets. Identical cubicles house her colleagues in long, pseudo-private rows. All the furniture is identical, though some of her colleagues have brought in photos from home, postcards of exotic places and inspirational sayings to personalise their space. Her cubicle is at the back of the department, to afford her the privacy necessary for someone in her position. Someone who takes and makes confidential calls, someone who is privy to high-level decisions and results. Cora's desk has one framed photo of her husband and children. She doesn't like clutter or mess. She'd prefer nothing but her computer and phone.

She is the manager of a small team who sit around her in various poses of industry. They talk on the phone, they type, they stare at their computer screens, they chew their nails.

A woman approaches Cora, smiling. Her teeth are too large for her mouth and her lips too thin to cover them. She is always smiling. Cora looks up and smiles back, it's impossible not to. The woman hands Cora a mug of coffee. Her nails are long and immaculately polished a deep red colour. Her hair is a shiny blonde helmet, expensively cut and coloured. She isn't married, or at least wears no rings and has never mentioned a husband to Cora. A burgundy wrap-around dress shows off her freckled bosom.

'Thanks, Hannah, you're a star.'

'You looked like you needed a coffee. How's it all going?'

'Good, thank you. Just finishing the report for Dave and then I'm all done for the day. You? How was your weekend? Weren't you going on a hen do?'

'Oh my God! It was mental! Jenny got completely shit-faced and ended up snogging the face off some bloke in a bar. Then Cathy threw up in the taxi back to the hotel. Honestly, I haven't been in such a state since college.'

Cora laughs, 'You're a lunatic, Hannah! I don't how you do it.'

'Hard work and determination...and lots of practice! Right, I'll leave you to it and finish off my spreadsheets for old Saggy Pants before he starts shouting the odds and reports me to you.'

'You do that. Thanks for the coffee, I owe you one.' Cora leans back and straightens her grey, pleated skirt, smoothing it over her thighs before sliding her feet back into her shoes. This version of Cora is fun and well-liked. She is good at her job and is kind to her staff. Everyone likes Cora at JJ Beadle Ltd and she likes them back. She watches everyone around her, she works with them most days and yet she knows nothing about them. They're strangers who laugh and joke with each other. They go out and get drunk on a Friday together and moan about the boss and their crappy bonuses at Christmas. She turns back to her computer and reads through her work, putting stupid thoughts out of her mind. Here she is free to think only of herself, to exist in the air-conditioned vacuum of financial services, completing her tasks, achieving her carefully set, line-manager agreed objectives. Emotions are not required here, in fact they are discouraged. Unprofessional. Here all the rules are explicit; Cora knows exactly who she is.

She stands up and walks the short distance to her boss's office. Three of its walls are glass and she can see him sitting at his desk, talking to someone on the phone. He is tall and slim, with expressive, elegant hands. He has a short neat moustache and some of the others joke that he looks like a pervert. Cora imagines him trimming it every morning with a pair of tiny nail scissors, snipping away at the coarse hairs around his mouth and nose, his little finger cocked high. His suit is impeccably pressed but he always smells of stale tobacco smoke. The ban on smoking is torture for Dave MacAdam and he usually conducts his meetings standing outside on the pavement with a cigarette between his teeth, regardless of the weather. He looks up and, seeing Cora at his door, he waves her in as he puts the phone down.

'Cora, to what do I owe the pleasure?' His face folds up into a smile exposing his yellowed teeth.

'Well, Dave, I'm thinking it's time to come back to work full-time. I'm grateful that you gave me the part-time hours, but I need to come back now, if that's possible. What do you think?' She remains standing, her heels pressing into the nylon carpet. One doesn't sit without invitation in Dave MacAdam's office.

'Are you sure?' He leans back in his chair and stretches his arms out in front of him, tugging at the cuffs of his shirt. 'What about the family?'

'What do you mean?'

'I mean how do they feel about it? Will you be able to manage working full-time with the children and everything? I know how hard it can be.' He presses his bottom lip up under his moustache as if confirming it is still there.

Cora shifts her weight from one foot to the other, her body swaying slightly, rocked by the urge to throw something at him.

'It's my decision actually and I've decided to work full-time and I'm absolutely sure that I can manage.' She wants to both hit him and beg him to let her come back. He has the power to save her and the family.

'Of course, of course.' Dave blinks quickly in defence, his eyes twitching. 'I'll speak to HR, but we'd be delighted to have you back at full capacity, I'm sure.'

'Thank you. That would be great. Will you let me know?'

'Yes, indeed.' He nods and turns towards his screen, ending the conversation.

She looks at her watch. She has forty minutes left before she has to go home. Her stomach contracts into a small hard ball. She has to return soon, it's expected: more than that, it's required. It's her turn to cook. Her turn to collect the children from the childminder. She walks back to her desk, panic flows like an electric current around her body. She must be responsible, a mother and wife. That's what she is. More importantly, it's what she chose to be, not knowing just what the choice might demand. A thin line of sweat gathers above her lip. An email pings in her inbox: it's from her husband. She stares at it unopened for a few seconds before clicking it open.

Hey Darling,

Fancy a takeaway tonight? If you feed the little 'uns, I'll grab noodles and that curry you like from the Thai on my way home.

Love you x

She blinks in the light of the screen. He is trying to help her, doing little things like this to make life easier for her. She knows she should go home, pick up the children and make them dinner. She could make a stew or something like that. She could have it ready for him when he gets in, have the children bathed and ready for bed. She could be a good wife and mother. She could be a success. She must try. But she can't. She can't begin to think about how to achieve all of that without something going very wrong. She could drop a pan, or slice herself with a knife, she might burn the children or set fire to the kitchen. She emails back:

That sounds like a plan.

C x

She leans back and watches the second hand on her watch erase the time she has left.

In the women's washroom she stands and washes her hands, rubbing the soap into her skin, rinsing under the tap and then starting again, squeezing the thick pink liquid out of the dispenser. She watches herself in the mirror, confronting herself, like a liar evading the truth, shifty-eyed. The lighting is cold and hard and bounces in sharp angles off the mirror and stainless steel fittings. She looks tired and pale, her hair dull and needing a cut. Her thin brown hair falls in not-quite-curls to her shoulders, her brown eyes are round and short-lashed, her nose has an uptilt at its tip, a small bump that she hates. Her mascara collects in dried black crumbs around her eyes. She rubs at them, making the smears worse. A group of women walk into the room talking and laughing and gather at the mirror next to her.

'You alright, Cora? Long time no see.'

Startled, Cora looks across at the woman who spoke. 'Hi Sonja. Sorry I didn't see you there. Yes, thanks, all good. You?'

'Yeah, all good. Girls, this is Cora from Comms, she was my boss before I moved up with you lot!'

The other women nod and smile. They are polite as could be, sweetness and light. Sonja leans in towards the mirror, applying lip-gloss with a small brush.

'How's it going up there?' Cora asks, shaking her hands.

'I love it! I miss you all, obviously, but I love it.' Sonja rubs her lips together before pouting in the mirror and then turns back to Cora. 'We're going out for a glass or two of wine. Fancy coming along?'

Cora hesitates. 'I'd love to, but I have to get back for the kids. Another time maybe.' The knot in her stomach twists tighter. She has no choice, no space to move, she is trapped. One wrong move from her could spell disaster. She is a potential murderer, one bad decision and that would be it. The other women spread lipstick over their mouths and use corners of tissue paper to tidy the edges, carefully outlining their lips. It's mouths that she notices. Cora is surrounded by mouths. Like a mother bird, precarious on a nest edge, she is surrounded by open, hungry mouths. Mouths that tell, ask, shout, demand, whisper – mouths that swallow whole.

'Ah, yeah. Another time, always welcome. You're lucky, you are. I can't wait to get married and have kids. I need to find someone who'll have me first though!' She laughs loudly, her head tipped back showing the dark fillings in her back teeth, the other women laugh too. 'They alright, your little ones?'

'Yes, thank you.' Cora smiles, her lips stretched thin, and picks up her bag. 'Have a good time tonight.'

'Oh OK then, will do!' Sonja says as Cora abruptly turns and leaves the rest of the women adjusting their make-up and hair in the mirror. The door swings shut behind her. She strides out of the building, through the heavy glass doors and past security, pushing past the men and women crowding the street, she has to be quick. Her heavy bag jolts against her shoulder and thigh, her shoes pinch her feet and her head pounds but she can't slow down. She must be on time.

There are no delays, no inconsiderate suicides sticky on the tracks, no leaves on the line. So far so good. She even manages to get a seat on the crowded train. She will arrive at the child-minder as expected, punctual and responsible. She leans over and picks up an abandoned newspaper from the seat opposite. She looks at the pictures but doesn't read the articles. Her head swims, the movement of the carriage making her feel sicker than she did before. The train stops at a station and the carriage empties. A thickset man in jeans and royal blue football shirt sits down in the seat opposite. He catches her eye for a second before crossing his arms across his chest, leaning his head back on the seat and closing his eyes. His knuckles are coated with a grey substance and his jeans are dirty. His face and head are clean-shaven, exposing skin as shiny and pink as a boiled ham, but black hair covers his arms and sprouts above the neckline of his shirt. He snores softly. Cora watches him sleep, his hairy arms curled around his belly. He has a lion tattoo on his forearm, its sharp teeth on show.

He grunts and shifts in his seat and scratches his face without waking. He reminds her of her father. Short and strong, with a hard-faced look. She leans her head back against the seat. Opposite, he opens his legs, spreading himself across his seat to get comfortable the way only a man can. She envies his ability to sleep like this, like a baby, sleeping anywhere the need takes him, entirely unafraid.

Like her father used to settle into his armchair. The brown velour chair placed just so, with the best view of the TV and closest to the gas fire. The chair reserved just for him, her mother ready to bring him anything he needed, jumping up for his cups of tea, his beer, his scotch. Fetching his slippers, bringing him the paper, while he snored through the football or the wildlife programmes he'd chosen for them all to watch. Sometimes Cora would climb up onto his lap and snuggle up with him, leaning back against his heavy body. Her mother left alone on the frilly sofa, a bag of sweets at her side, her feet tucked up under her, reading a magazine.

Cora gathers herself up, pulling her self in tighter, getting ready to go home.

I have secrets too. But it doesn't matter, because even though you are lying there next to me, pretty in your cotton nightgown, a pinch of fluff caught on your lip, you are not there. I've no idea where you are, what you think about. I have no idea what to do. I feel like I'm a time traveller, reporting back from the past in order to secure you to our present. An anachronism, I drift between there and now, trying to find my wife in amongst all the stories we create around ourselves. I wonder if I've made us up, if all the memories are false, everything lost. You wouldn't be interested in my secret, I know that: you are only interested in the children and their day-to-day adventures. You're wholly a mother. Perhaps that's it, you're only a mother now, you've ceased to be my wife. Something has slipped away. Something I just about see in the periphery of my vision but can never focus on.

I watched you picking at your food this evening, as if you were rifling through it for something disgusting or dangerous, as though you didn't trust the meal I'd made you. Imagine that. As if I could ever hurt you. It was like watching a hostage consume their first captive meal, picking through to find razor blades or ground glass or poison. It seems that nothing I do is enough, whatever I try to do for you, whether it's cooking or cleaning up or buying you a silly little treat to try and make you smile, you just look disappointed.

What I want to say is that I am fucking trying, trying so hard to be everything that you and the kids need me to be. You know, I am so afraid of losing you, that you'll disappear for good and take the children with you. I will do anything to make this work. Just tell me what I need to do. You and the kids – you'll always belong to each other. You'll always be a unit. No matter what happens, the courts would give you custody. A man is always on the outside with no real access to that closeness, that bond between mother and child. And I can't be the man left alone, the man who only sees his kids every other weekend, living in a small flat, my life cut up into pieces. I know how it goes, I've seen it. You get the house, the kids, half my pension. I get meals for one, sitting in the pub on my own and Christmas at my sister's. I get to watch my wife with another man, in another life. I can't be him. I won't. I can only imagine there is another man, but you wouldn't do that, would you? Would you do that? Would you let another person into our marriage? What else could it be? And I'm too afraid to ask, too afraid to hear the answer. I'm trapped into this silence.

You turn over and face me, blinded by sleep. You don't see me, lying here looking at you, listening to you, listening out for the kids who'll stir any minute now and need feeding. We need a holiday. Just the two of us. Like the one we took in Cornwall, when we were first together, in that tiny house. The one with the low ceilings that I smashed my head on over and over again, and the short bed that my feet dangled from. You laughed and said I was a giant in the house of small lovers. The kitchen window was tied shut with string and the sofa covered with dog hairs. There was no heating except the open fire in the sitting room. We fucked like Trojans there. I made you come with my tongue and you said that it was the first time for you. I felt like a god. Yes, we should go away, just the two of us. My parents could have the kids.

I want you to remember how I taught you to skim stones, and when you tied bacon rinds to the end of a piece of string and went crabbing, collecting the sharp-clawed little bastards in a bucket. I wish you would remember. I wish you would remember what it's like to be happy with me, because the memory might become a reality. That can happen.

I watched you smoking, looking out to sea, a strand of your hair stuck to your cheek. Later I twisted a tissue to a point and removed the sand from between your toes because you didn't like the grit on your skin. I warmed your jumper on the radiator in the morning before you got up. You made tea in those chipped enamel mugs. You seemed so tiny, and me so big and brutal next to you. You ran naked into the freezing sea late at night, shouting at me to come in and I stood on the shore laughing at you, gorgeous you, and I wrapped you in a towel when you emerged laughing and shivering at the same time.

I asked you about your parents and your childhood, and you told me that your dad was wonderful and funny, that your mother was a good mum, always there. Nothing more. You never mentioned friends or old boyfriends from the past, though I've seen pictures of you smiling, in a crowd of other young smiling people, with your arm around someone. You keep your secrets close, Cora.

We lit candles, we drank wine, we began to smell of each other. We did all the things you're supposed to do to prove love, to prove that you're falling in love and making all the right memories which we will use to shore up against the future, against drudgery and loss. Memories, which should act like flotation devices upon which we'll pile our hopes and plans. The memories that I'm relying on now. You wore a green parka with patches at the elbows. You looked like a skinny boy in your jeans and wellies. Your grey sweatshirt that hung over your frame. So unlike my blonde mother and sister, with their tennis obsession and outfits for every occasion. Your freckles darkening over your upturned nose. So different from the polished office version of yourself.

I told you all about my family and you listened intently, cradling a glass of wine in your hand. You always seemed so interested in me. I told you about Sally and how protective of me she was, my little sister, training to be a doctor, part-time tennis coach at my mother's club. Engaged to David, another medic, just back from Pakistan where they'd volunteered for the Red Cross. I told you about my mum and dad, his accountancy business and mother's social events and charity work. All facts that sum them up. Good people, my people. Now I'm pretty sure you don't like them. But I can't think why. They've only ever been good and kind to both us and the kids. But back then, sitting there on the sofa, my arm slung across the back in a half-embrace, your legs tucked under you so you took up hardly any space, I couldn't wait for you to meet them. I wanted you to be part of our family: I knew then that I would marry you.

My parents used to have sex a lot. God, what a funny thing to remember like that. Sally and I used to hear them at night. My mother confided in Sally that our father was very highly-sexed and that she couldn't quite manage all his desires. I can't imagine Sally's response, whether she hooted with laughter as she always does when she's embarrassed or whether she affected her furrowed brow and vaguely professional air. Sally never told me her response; only that mother was relieved that age had calmed him down.

Once I saw them, actually saw them at it. It was hideous, as you would imagine. Christ, it's still so vivid! It was the afternoon and I'd been out with Reuben and Nicolas setting rabbit snares in the woods, we were obsessed with hunting at the time, and I came down the drive and round the side of the house towards the terrace. I was late and covered in dirt and so was sneaking about to avoid my mother. I was around ten I think, still at St. George's Prep, certainly still pretty innocent.

And there they were in the conservatory, his pink wobbly bum going like the clappers, her legs waving about in the air. I didn't know what to do. Did I go back the way I came, hoping they wouldn't see me? Or walk in on them? Or walk past the conservatory to the French doors of the dining room? I can't really place how I felt all that time ago, but I know that I wanted them to stop. I remember that very clearly, that it had to stop. That it made me feel sick and that I never really felt the same way about my mother again, if I'm honest. They both seemed changed, removed from me. Not my parents, just some adults, not quite strangers, subject to ugly convulsions. Perhaps I was jealous that I wasn't part of their bond as a couple. That I was on the outside. Rejected. That they existed without Sally and me. Maybe it's just revolting for a child to see the sex act. It does look pretty bloody dreadful. So I made a noise and stomped towards the conservatory as if I'd not seen them and opened the door, while they jumped up and straightened their clothes and my father started wittering about knocking before entering rooms. I remember that I was pleased by their discomfiture. It was never mentioned by them again. Just one of those things. But I've never told anyone about it. Not my friends, not even my sister. I wonder if I will ever tell you.

You once said that speaking, talking too much was a sign of weakness, almost as if words themselves were the problem, not the person speaking, just the words. You said that it was all pretend, artifice. You said that everything was artificial – an illusion – that words confirmed. I remember that, very clearly. I thought you were bonkers: beautiful, young and bonkers. Just young, I suppose. But now, thinking about what you said, I wonder how can we know ourselves, or each other without speaking, without confidences. We are our words, aren't we? Even sharing the incidental, banal stuff that you think is pointless feels good to me. I want you to know me, to know all my silly thoughts and the events of my day. Even things as boring as getting a parking ticket or what George said in a meeting to embarrass himself or who said what to whom at lunch and how long the queue was in Waitrose and what the old woman in front of me said to the checkout girl and I want to know what you think about and what you do each day, and who annoys you and who makes you laugh. I want to know what you long for, what you're afraid of. What makes you laugh when you're alone. We can't just talk about Patch and Jess. I want to hear you, know you and that isn't artificial. You're wrong about that. It's real, utterly real. It's silence that ruins love, not talking. Love is fed on words. It's your silence that hurts me the most. Your secrets.

The large clock on the wall in the sitting room marks out time. Cora sits on the sofa, a book open in her lap. The house is quiet: empty. She is supposed to enjoy this emptiness, revel in the depths of the peace, the space, as if it were a hot spring she could sink herself into. As her husband left the house with the children he kissed her and said, 'Have a little time to yourself, Darling. It'll do you good. Perhaps open a bottle of wine or something. Go for a walk, watch a film. We'll be back around seven...OK, take care. We love you.'

Sitting there, she feels time should open up before her, as if a gate were thrown wide revealing an expanse that she could disappear inside, but it doesn't. It closes off, constricts as sure as a snare. They have gone for the day: he has driven them over to his sister's, where they will play with their cousins, shouting, dirty-faced yelps of excitement, running garden dirt through his patient sister's house; she is a doting mother, their aunt, her sister-in-law. His parents will be there – the grandparents, the heads of the family. There will be absolute harmony. She won't be missed, she is sure of that.

Everything is demarcated, a territory, a place, the family, love, even sex. All relationships are territorial, marked off, divided from all the others, outsiders, instating privacy. There is no such thing as time, only geometry, topography, the delineation of words, shared interests, history. The only unity Cora can understand is spatial. She consists of spaces, gaps between matter. She takes up space on the sofa. Breathing.

He drove off with the children, strapped into the solid family car, a bag of grapes on the back seat between them and a CD of nursery rhymes in the player. He backed out of the drive expertly, barely looking over his shoulder, the dark hairs on his large hands shadowing the tanned flesh as if he were a sketch, a quick pencil drawing of a man, capable and fixed in his pose, before reaching his left hand out of sight, pushing the gear into drive and pulling away quickly, casting her a wave of his hand through the rear windscreen. He began the journey of forty or so miles into the next county and into his past lives, his childhood haunts, the sites of teenage cigarettes and broken windows, rugby matches, summer balls and girls kissed.

She looks at the room around her, the muted cream-coloured walls, the rows of books on the shelves, the family photos – smiles pressed flat, timeless, dead – the striped rug her mother had bought for them, the fireplace that was never lit, always clean, never dirtied by ash or burnt embers, always cool to the touch. A polite room, tasteful. The book lays still in her lap, its yawning silence unreadable, the black type stuttering across the page, minute wounds on the paper; she closes it shut. There is no point in trying to read, no point in attempting to follow the breadcrumb trails of her thoughts. She puts the book back on the shelf and walks into the kitchen.

It's clean, as he left it. Wiping down each surface after making breakfast, the children eating cereal, legs swinging under the table, their spoons tapping against the bottom of the bowls with mechanical regularity as if they were small workers on an assembly line, heads bent over a fiddly task, whilst she slept in, too warm in her guilty bed. She wonders how she could possibly inhabit the empty house: without the family there she feels as if she is destined to only wait for their presence, as if she were programmed to spring into life when they returned only to slow to a stop with their absence, like a fairground automaton. How had she existed before the family came into being? She can't remember. This family she had brought into being was erasing her, slowly, fading her out, till she was only recognisable as one of its parts, a component that was no longer necessary. But of course she had existed, had been real without them. She was the young woman laughing in photos half-hidden around the house, surrounded by friends, old lovers, spaces that weren't defined by others' needs, only by her wishes. It seems that these memories are treacherous, her previous existence a betrayal of the family now, a past that undermines the foundations of the present, like a swarm of fat little grubs, chewing through the supporting walls. She can almost hear the grinding of miniscule teeth.

Walking out to the garden she catches sight of herself in the small mirror by the French doors. She knows that she isn't as attractive as her husband's previous girlfriends, had even overheard her mother-in-law once claim relief that the children looked like their side of the family and not Cora's. This was something she had never mentioned to her husband, but it corroded her, this thin acid of insecurity. She was not good enough, not good enough. But he'd chosen her; she supposed she should find comfort in that fact. Kindly, politely, he loves her. Though believing in an absolute love is as stupid as believing in fairies or God. There's always a lie hidden somewhere. He was hardly likely to confess that he wanted to fuck their pretty young neighbour, or his line manager or secretary or the girl in the petrol station who once admired his suit, but no doubt he did. So all she has is trust, a mutual pretence: what you don't know can't hurt you. He would never know that she wanted him to fuck her with another man, or that she owed thousands on a credit card, or that sometimes she wished him and the children dead, for example. The lies preserve the life they have made. Honesty would kill it, tear it apart and leave it scattered for the scavengers.

In the garden, she looks without seeing, standing still, her pale hands limp at her side. The lawn needs mowing. A purple peony bush is shedding its petals next to a small thicket of lavender. Her daughter's toys are scattered, garish on the grass, the harsh plastics in primary colours polluting the calm green. Cora's shirt is missing a button. She's not the type to sew a button back on, preferring not to halt the disintegration of things; she just replaces, buys new. An inherent decadence, or just laziness, but then perhaps laziness is a form of decadence, a withdrawing of effort and will: a refusal to pursue, indulging in the luxury of passivity. She walks slowly up the garden, its basic oblong conforming to suburban planning, the straight lines interrupted by the curved beds planted with untidy shrubs; flowers punctuate the space here and there, giving pause for a moment. Neither of them had bothered much with the garden: it was untended, left to its own devices and the unruly attentions of the children.

An apple tree grows at the end of the lawn, its branches thick and fertile. As she approaches it throws black shadows across her face, bars of cool shade in the bright sunlight. Apples hang from the branches, a hundred red-green orbs studding the bark, visible through the thick leaves. It seems magical, producing, fruiting without their aid or husbandry, cajoled by bees and wandering insects, silently maternal in the garden. Under the tree the grass is pocked with rotten fallen fruit, the apple's flesh softened and melting into the soil like soap, the harvest squandered. Fodder for wasps, which then sting her children. The sticky sweet waste appals her. She has always bought their apples, neat and green, wrapped in cellophane, unsullied by nature, almost as if manufactured, not grown. When here, if she made the effort, if she could trust them, were more apples than they could eat. She feels sick, her stomach rising towards her mouth, sick at the waste, and sick at the sight of the brown mush, the bright optimism of the apples corrupted by dirt and rot.

She's wasting time, standing there crying over fallen apples. The neighbours might see. They'll see her stupidity and ugliness. She wipes her face on her hands, spreading her fingers wide over her cheeks. Silly: there is no one to see. No one but her out in the gardens. What did it matter if she cried or not? I should stop wasting time. I'm alright. I'm alright. She stands. She tries to think. She ought to do something.

Back in the kitchen she finds the key to the shed in a drawer. She rarely visits the little structure at the bottom of the garden.

It seems remote and inhabited by mystery and danger. She strides towards it, stepping over toys and apples. The key turns easily in the lock, there is nothing to it. Simple, easy, just a quick turn. Inside, it's ordinary, half full with tools and beach toys, her husband's collection of vinyl records. The mystery, the glamour of trepidation has come to nothing. She picks up a pair of gardening gloves and a trowel from a shelf and shuts the door.

Kneeling, she digs in the soil of the flower beds, the whistles and peeps of the birds repeating around her as if on a mechanical loop – what are they saying to each other, that can be said over and over again? She fears repetition. Doesn't trust its reassurances. A golden strand, a centipede runs through her gloved fingers, as dextrous as a card trick. She shivers, glad of the protection of the gloves. Flicks it off into the soil. Proud of her bravery. She can do this, she can be good, she can service the family and home. She digs up a plant, easing it from the earth, guarding the stem and leaves from breaking, her hands tender against the limp green. She cups the bulge of soil clamped by the roots in her palm, easing the snarled pale fronds from the ball, softly teasing out the congestion. She watched her mother do this hundreds of times. Her mother's garden receiving all her loving attentions.

She wonders what she ought to do with it. Where it might go. She moves to another part of the garden, closer to the shed and digs it a hole, the soil dry and powdery, collapsing back like sand as she digs. She presses the plant into its new space. Leaning back on the grass, the machinery of its leaves filtering the light, growing, converting, remaking, renewing; her fingers drowse in the blades. A train hisses at the end of the garden, city bound. Shaking the house. She has barely affected the garden; it doesn't look any different at all. She puts away the gloves and trowel. She is useless.

Clean laundry hangs from the line by the house; pressing her cheek against the folds, she feels for damp. She reaches up, unclipping the pegs her husband had placed earlier, his efficient hands deft and cheerful. Always cheerful. She imagines him, playing with the children, hanging washing, cleaning while she slept, her dark sleep of escape into which she retreats every night, always tired. Folding the laundry over her arm, she works, helping, taking part in the chore. She can do it too. She can be capable. He will see that she has helped.

Spiders have spun webs across the line, the delicate threads crystalline in the sunlight. Her husband has hung one of Patch's t-shirts over one, destroying it, the torn silks sticking to the blue cotton, the broken web suddenly ordinary, tattered and reduced. Cora carefully unpegs the shirt, looking for the spider. Her entire body tenses, alert to the small danger lurking. She's sure it will have gone. It must have gone. As Cora folds the shirt the spider emerges from the fabric, running across her hand, its brown mottled body lagging behind the pointed legs, as pointed as needles; she shrieks, dropping the laundry, slapping her left hand against her right, moaning, brushing it off, looking for it, frightened it's still on her, in her clothes, concealed, waiting to emerge. Her scalp itches immediately as if covered with crawling insects.

She rushes through the house and up the stairs to the shower, at every step feeling the spider palpating her skin with its two front legs, or injecting her with venom, or crawling into her ear, or climbing inside her underwear. In the bathroom she drops her clothes into the bath in case the spider crawls from the folds and invades the house. She stands under the water, hearing the noise of the pipes – the workings of the house – her hair in streaks fastened against her flesh, as she scrubs and scrubs. She remembers a time when she wasn't afraid. When she had made pets of garden snails, and caught tiny frogs, new-legged, fresh from the pond. The stick insects that she'd fed privet, living their unmoving lives in her pink bedroom. And spiders she'd catch under a drinking glass to release back into the garden, to the relief of her grateful mother. Her father proud of her bravery, of her curiosity, large-eyed, her four-year-old self pulling off the spindled legs of crane-flies, leaving them de-legged, de-winged, just body, a fleck of brown on the patio like a blade of dried grass. And earlier, gloved, she hadn't panicked at the centipede. She'd coped.

And now this fear. She leans back against the tiled wall, the water stippling her pink skin. The flesh on the top of her thighs is pale and softer than that on her arms, where the skin has coarsened from exposure to the sun. She rubs soap under her arms, across her breasts, her stomach, between and down her legs. All things change. But when had she become afraid of insignificant things? She can't remember. It's silly, a stupid fear. Her father would laugh, so would her son, perhaps even her husband. She feels calmer, embarrassed at her panic. Outside, she can hear children playing, the occasional car, dogs bark. There is nothing to be frightened of. Nothing at all. How stupid to be frightened of a spider. Stupid, stupid me. Stupid fucking me. She turns the temperature dial on the shower and forces herself to stand still as freezing cold water knifes her skin. Her body begins to shudder under the numbing slashes, her teeth chattering; but she continues to stand there, cleansing her fear, performing an excision. Her skin puckering in defence, contracting around her, pulling in tight. She turns the water off.

She dresses, pulling on a clean shirt and jeans, leaving the other clothes in the bath for her husband to inspect and declare safe. He will laugh, but he will do it for her; diligently checking for the villainous spider, as he seemingly does all things – gently, kindly. She must make amends. She must prove herself. Perhaps she should make dinner. But then maybe they will have eaten at the sister's and won't be hungry. She walks down the carpeted stairs, still looking for the spider, just in case it has fallen from her clothes as she ran upstairs to the bathroom. She could make something simple, perhaps a soup, or a quiche, with boiled potatoes and a salad. She could make something light, or something that could be refrigerated if they didn't want it, it needn't be a waste. She can't go back out into the threat of the garden, not now. There is still some time left before they are due home.

The sun is going down, that's hardly surprising, but she is surprised by how quickly her boon of free time has disappeared. The sudden shock of winter dark. Summer's almost over. With a turn of her wrist or press of her thumb she could switch something on and make something happen. She could change things immediately: in just touching an object she would alter it for good. She could master the room. She looks in the refrigerator, and pulls out eggs, onions and potatoes. A Spanish omelette would be simple enough, her thoughts extend from herself as if she is in conversation with someone else; she is incapable of being alone, but it's all she longs for.

Outside the weather changes. Particles of rain scatter like grit across the patio and bounce off the glass of the skylights. Remembering the washing she runs to the door: the bright fabric shapes scattered on the grass are already blotched with water. She hesitates, her hand on the frame, not sure whether to push herself out into the garden or hold herself back. A spider could be lurking still, sheltered in the pink cotton folds of her daughter's knickers or tucked into the sleeve of a t-shirt. It may be watching her, hesitant in the doorway, her hands bracing her weight, her shadow dormant on the kitchen floor – it may be watching her. Its eyes fixed on her, as vigilant as a security camera or a good mother.

She turns, shutting the door. Turning the lock. Locking it out. She whisks eggs, slices potatoes, heats oil. A process. One thing after another. She enjoys the logic of cooking. Following the steps. Cora turns down the heat. Time has passed. Just minutes. She looks up at the clock. It is 6 pm. They will be back soon. She will belong to them again. The omelette will be cool, as it should be. She sits at the kitchen table, her hands resting on the wooden top.

She creates dark with the flick of a switch. They are still not home. Nine o'clock, two hours later than he said they'd be, an hour and a half later than bedtime. She sits in the dark. Still in the kitchen, listening to her own breathing. No key turning the lock of the front door. There are explanations, she is sure of that. Such as? Such as bad traffic; or staying later for supper; or perhaps he decided to stay over at his sister's, having drunk too much. She lifts the phone. He would've called by now. She thinks about calling his sister. She puts the phone down. Unsure of what to ask. Unsure that she wanted an answer. She tips the omelette into the bin. The dark quiet is placid. She's alone. Foetal. No bad news, yet. What would be bad news?

A simple movement, an over-steer, or not looking back in the mirror. That could've happened. And then? Then the car swerving, his panic, righting the wheel, the children asleep in the back of the car, unaware. The deceptively straight lines of the road buckling around them. A car behind, maybe a large expensive car, travelling too fast, clipping the back of them. Sending them spinning, a pirouette all the more graceful for her children's presence. Hitting another car, it smashing them in the side, that would cause the most damage. Her children being thrust against their restraining belts, fracturing ribs, cracking pelvises, smashing small internal organs. Bleeding. Glass everywhere. Metal penetrating soft tissues. The car they had all travelled in together many times completely transformed. The plastic dashboard crumpling on impact. And the smells; petrol, burning flesh, blood, churned soil. She moves to the sofa, sitting with two soft cushions either side of her, her feet tucked under her body. His head flopped on the wheel. His mouth gaping. The sounds: what would they hear? Screams, yes, and the impact, the excitement of metal refolding, bending, finding a new curve, glass scattering into little teeth. And being hit again, a second car. Blood like water. Plentiful. This one finishing the job. Dead. She exposed them to this. This finitude. By giving birth to them, allowing light and dark, breath, those collections of molecules that gathered together inside her. She produced this ending. She killed them. And now, finally, she thinks, she could love them

40

and treasure them. Visit them all at the cemetery with flowers. She could be a good mother. They would be safe. She would be safe. She could make no more mistakes. From the beginning, she knew how it would be.

Announced by headlights and the noise of the engine, the car pulls onto the drive. They're back, safe. They are back. Cora stands, makes herself walk to the door, open it and look out.

'There you are! I was expecting you all hours ago.' He walks in, Jessica asleep over his shoulder, Patrick being led stumbling, half-asleep.

'Sorry Darling, the motorway was madness, at a standstill.' He walks up the stairs. 'I'll just put them straight into bed.'

'And your phone? You couldn't call?'

'Cora, I was driving. I'm sorry. We're back now, all safe. I won't be a minute.'

She watches him go. The small children loose with sleep, alive, their blood pulses, gloating. Safe with their father. Real, right there, he holds them, carries them, their heat, their flesh, he walks up the stairs with his children. She stands, unreal, surplus, watching at the foot of the stairs, feeling nothing, which is everything. He performs his role with exacting quiet. He is the perfect husband and father. What a performance. Cora walks back into the kitchen and vomits into the sink.

I never had any doubts about us. Never. Not even in the beginning. I knew you were the one I wanted to marry. Maybe it's crazy, but I just knew that I wanted to be with you for the rest of my life. You were the woman I wanted to wake up with every day, go to bed with every night. I could imagine being the best person I could be with you. Not that my old mates understood. They were still drinking and shagging and playing rugby on Sundays, though none of them were particularly young. Do you remember that stupid joke Gerry told us when we announced our engagement?

'How'd you make your girlfriend stop sucking your cock?

You marry her.'

Well, that about summed up their attitude. They're no different even now they're all married with kids. They still scan the room for totty, sizing up the women's tits and up for a shag if they think they could get away with it. The last time I saw them that's all they talked about: this bird and that bird, who was doing what and with whom, how to get away with it; hotel rooms at lunch time, conferences in the Far East, car parks that have dark but busy corners, slutty air stewardesses that make the red-eye more comfortable, web pages where married women advertise for discreet daytime sex, having a secret mobile phone just for your bit on the side. But not me. You're all I need, all I want. You and the kids. That should be enough, shouldn't it? For anyone. I'm a good man, Cora. I try to be.

Friends fall away anyhow, you have less and less in common, forget to call, forget to invite them over, and vice versa – the invites stop coming. Things change, people move on. Especially once we got together; I saw less and less of my mates, not just because I was spending time with you, but because they didn't ask me to go out so much. You never liked them anyway. It was a shame, but you make new friends, at least you should. I always thought we'd make lots of friends, once we were married, *you know, other couples and then later, via the kids, from NCT classes, with all the babies born around the same time so you can share worries and babysitting duties. I left it all to you – my mother was always in charge of that stuff, socialising and organising dinner parties and sending the Christmas cards. I realise now it's not fair to do that. To leave all the responsibility to you. Bit chauvinistic perhaps. But I imagined that we'd be those people who hosted great dinner parties, with good food and long boozy conversations, that the kids would have their little pals over and play in the garden and you would have a circle of friends who were mothers too. You'd have coffee mornings and the same group would meet on a Saturday night for dinner and us husbands would be there and we'd form a new group of friends, a group we'd get old with, go on group holidays with and have evenings out together.*

I used to have these images of us. Of what our lives would be like. Like I had a pictorial map of our future. I carried these images everywhere, about every aspect of our lives. I don't think there's anything wrong in having expectations. It's good to know what you want, what you're striving for. How else do you succeed in life?

I wonder if you'd remember that furniture shop we used to look in and pretend we could afford to buy from. It smelt of vanilla and fresh coffee, with the scary shop assistant dressed head to toe in expensive black. We saved and saved and finally went to choose a dining table and all the way there, I thought about how the table we chose would be a huge part of our lives. That all that money spent on a solid oak eight-seater would be worth every penny for all the fun we'd share around it. That it would last and last and it would bear the weight of all our family suppers and Christmases and birthdays and dinner parties and drinks parties and games nights. That the table would see the kids grow up and leave then come back with their own kids. I imagined that we'd never need to replace it, that it would become

43

a member of the family, almost. One of those familiar objects that reassure you, that remind you of your family's constancy.

You laugh at this stuff, I know. But I think like that. I have a vision of what our life should be and I do my best to live up to it. You say I'm a sucker, an advertising man's dream. Maybe, maybe I am. But I want so much from our lives. I want money in the bank and friends and holidays and the kids to grow up happy and strong. I want us to have nice things and a nice home. I want our families to be happy. I want to gather all these things and experiences up and keep them close by. I want you, I want to fuck you on that dining table again, I want you to come on to me, to initiate sex. I want you to want me again. I want you to look at me and see me.

You take a deep breath and then sigh as you exhale. You sleep deeply, you always have. Though sometimes you frown and I wonder what you're dreaming, who you're angry with in your sleep. You seem more alive in your sleep, as if your dreams captivate you more than real life, than us, than me.

A moth has spread itself out in a corner of the lampshade, forming a dusty V shape; the dull brown symmetry is reassuring. So ordinary, but I like that we aren't alone in this room, I feel as if the moth connects us to the outside world. That's like something you'd say. I catch myself doing that sometimes, talking like you, using your little phrases and peculiarities. Like I'm becoming you. Someone's not quite turned a tap off. Drip, drip, drip, ticking away time. Like a machine supplementing the clock. I should get up and turn it off. Wake the kids and leave you to your sleep. But I can't drag myself out of bed. I'm tired. I like lying here next to you. I want to stroke your body, touch you, lift your nightie over your thighs, look at your soft body, and pretend we are back where we used to be. That other place.

We don't have sex often enough. God, that seems harsh and crude. I don't want to hurt you. But we don't. I need to feel close to you. I need you, I need to be inside you, I need to know that we're still together, and not just still married, still in the same

*house, but together. Really together. I miss the intimacy, I miss
being wanted. I want to be touched, I want to be held, it's not
all about fucking, but what's so wrong with that anyway. I've
started taking longer showers and fantasising about you and me.
Sometimes I think about you and another woman touching each
other, kissing each other all over and I'm just watching. Standing
there in the corner of our room watching you suck on her breasts
as she touches your pussy. I want to watch you come as she licks
you and I want to see her push herself into your mouth, rubbing
herself on your lips, your tongue. Why do these fantasies feel like
acts of disloyalty? But they do. I feel guilty for thinking these
things. Terrible. But I need something. I'm not made of stone; I've
done nothing wrong. You must feel it too, unless you're finding
it elsewhere. That's what I'm afraid of, of course. You don't need
me. I'm not enough anymore. I can't understand why though. I've
done nothing wrong, Cora.*

    *I notice things now. Things I'd never have before. Like yesterday
in a meeting with George and the other heads of departments. All
sat around the conference table. Our notepads and pens in front
of us next to our BlackBerries. My shirtsleeves rolled up. The
secretary bringing us tea and coffee. Watching Mike from Sales
give a presentation, his hair suddenly darker than usual, his
grey magicked away overnight, he's just got divorced, so, well...
The reassuring click of the mouse as Mick switches the slides, the
bottles of mineral water in the centre of the table, the glass wall
looking out into the open-plan office, the collection of cubicles
where my team sit, right outside my office. Just like any other
midweek management meeting. Nothing out of the ordinary.
The new Marketing manager, Amanda, was opposite me, taking
notes. I've met her before, and she seems nice enough, nothing
special, good at her job, has a nice voice. Wears a wedding ring,
has photos of small children on her desk. Married, a mother.
Nothing more. But yesterday during the meeting I noticed she'd
left a smudge of pink lipstick on her coffee mug, she seemed
embarrassed about it and I watched as she rubbed it off with*

her thumb as she spoke, smearing it further across the porcelain. And I got hard. That was all there was to it. And all there will ever be. But it happened. And now I'm a different man to the one I thought I was.

He's lying in bed, the small lamp on her side still on. His back towards her, head on the pillow, his ear vulnerable and translucent against his dark hair. Long ago, his mother would've gazed at him, mesmerised by his fragility. She'd loved him. Warm and damp in his cradle, merely human, not yet a man or even really a boy; she'd have leant over him, cooing her perfect love and attention. Now he was adult and dirtied and his mother was old and surely exhausted by all that loving. Beyond it. Degraded. Though the older woman still performed some version of love that was little more than possession and he loves back, easily, lightly, he loves his mother, the children, her.

Cora undresses in the half-light. Avoiding the sight of her own body, she stares at her husband. At the smooth skin, his body unmarked by the addition of the children, except for the dark bags under his eyes. He snores, and turning onto his back, farts, still sleeping, ignorant of his humiliation. She can't bear to look at him, so turns away. His unguarded self, tender and open to penetration, embarrasses her. He is an embarrassment. Revealed and vulnerable. She's reminded of seeing a woman fall down, skidding on a dropped sandwich, her entire body mass perched on the twin pinnacles of her high heels. The poor woman, in a shopping centre, glamorous, lip-sticked, short-skirted, falling to her knees, and others there all shopping too, with bags hanging from push-chairs, overloaded, laughing at her behind their hands, and just one or two stepping forward to help. But Cora couldn't look, she hurried by, her own cheeks flushed, disgusted by the ridiculous woman's shame. Perhaps not looking is the greater kindness.

Sliding into the bed, she moves slowly, carefully to avoid waking him. Gingerly lying back against her pillow. Her head heavy, the scalp itching. She hopes she's not caught nits from the children again, small children with their inevitable little parasites. Threadworms; tapeworms; nits; fleas; scabies; ringworm: they've had them all. A car ambles by, probably loaded with teenagers, red-faced, horny, dangerous; the sound attacks the window like weather. Music, or something like, but with all the emphasis on the bass, heavy sounds, stricken, like a dead weight.

He stirs next to her, turning over, his arm draping over her body. Smacking his lips like a hungry animal in a cartoon show. She closes her eyes, pretending sleep. No such luck, he puckers forward, a habit, lips extended like limbs, probing her cheek, testing the skin, analysing responses, moving closer to her mouth. Kissing her, pressing his lips against hers, still half-asleep, but rousing, she can feel his penis twitching against her leg. He hasn't brushed his teeth; his tongue, when it finds hers, tastes like a rancid vegetable. She shifts, not quite shrugging him off but maybe suggesting in that small movement her lack of enthusiasm. He presses on, misinterpreting, or not even feeling her move.

He keeps up the kissing, a tight pucker that resists; that defends the dark scramble of his head. It's not the kind of kiss that she likes, but then she can't remember ever receiving the kiss she might like. None of her lovers have kissed her well – there were John's fast pecks tap tapping on her lips, David's hollow sucking, several anonymous exchanges, smeared, in the dark – all hard work. All just in the mind. Really, if you think about it, it's just a matter of taste, and that can be reconditioned. You can get used to anything. You should at least try. He moves on top of her, his legs between hers, a promise of space. Still kissing, the mouth, then the neck, now the breasts, firm, precise kisses. Clean kisses, kisses that stay inside the lines, obedient. Nothing sloppy or juicy about them. Neatly declared on the ledger of her body, no excess, no arrears, everything in order. He inserts himself inside her, first tongue, then penis, moving carefully. She should try harder, receive him graciously, relieved and happy to have him and the children safely home. He is

48

gentle and eager to please. She should be pleased. She should work to please.

Looking down through the gap between their bodies she catches sight of his skin, unmarked and firm, pressing her down and then relieving her, pressing and relieving, repeat, repeat, repeat. She sees her disaster of a body, pads of fat collapsing from her hips into the bed, her belly judders, unkempt, purple stretch-marks like a child's scribble run up beyond her navel. She looks away, up at his face, his expression comic, hovering above her, a pale moon too close for comfort, his breath foul. She puts her arms around him. I must try, at least. His lips curl back over his teeth, his eyes close, a temporary blindness that permits later sight, he gapes, open-mouthed, head back, unabashed, like an imbecile. He is retarded by his pleasure. His arse cheeks clench, rigid, his whole body tensed, he comes, grunting, as she watches from the spectator's box inside her body, wishing she could join in rather than failing, always failing.

Morning, and she leans against the kitchen counter, her hip pressing into the chill marble, unyielding – the bone of her hip, the marble, the hard floor. Her hands wrapped around her warm cup. She looks without seeing at the garden beyond the French doors, at the photos stuck on the fridge, the family calendar. She is waiting for the sounds that mean the start of the day. The grunt of her husband as he walks to the bathroom, the small rhythm of the children's feet as they hurry down stairs, the rushing water of the shower, the quick slam of drawers as he chooses his socks, underwear, shirt, tie; his suits hang in his wardrobe. Sounds that should reassure – the machine of the family and its various components are working.

A child sits at the table, her feet dangling from the chair, the frill on her nightgown cavorting against her shin. She is a quiet child. Cora watches the girl sit at the table before turning and filling a plastic bowl with cereal and milk, obscuring the pattern of fairies dancing on the bottom. She places the bowl on the table and hands the child a spoon, before lighting a cigarette and turning back towards the counter. She shouldn't smoke. The child watches her. Everyone knows the rules. Mummy must not smoke. Usually she doesn't, she hasn't for months and months. But today she takes one of her emergency stash from behind the biscuit tin. Her head aches, her stomach lags, she couldn't sleep. She hasn't showered yet, and can still feel him sticky between her legs. His vibrant little swimmers, wasted, languishing in her knickers.

Cora shouts up the stairs, 'Patch! Are you dressed yet?' There will be a mumbled response, she knows without going up the stairs that the child will be playing with his macho super heroes. Their plastic pectoral muscles as big as pubescent breasts, they'll be flying through the air, saving the world, crash landing on his blue rug, splat, forever immortalised in petrochemical hues. 'I'm coming up the stairs now.' She steps, it takes no thought, this complicated manoeuvre, she takes a drag on the cigarette, and places the other hand on the rail. Pulling herself up. A foot on a stair, the knee bent and straightening, pushing up from the glutes, using the hamstrings, joints, muscles, tendons, the gristle of the body, all truth, it can't be argued with. There is no other way. Placing the next foot, and so on. You know how to walk up stairs. How it goes. These actions that we master and never think of again, until tragically our brains are bashed in by an accident or a stroke or old age and then it becomes a miraculous skill to relearn or let go, along with swallowing, speaking, eating, breathing. Making a mockery of any idea of a self that continues, anything as immutable as a Soul.

Her husband walks out onto the landing, as if making a stage entrance. 'Smoking? What's going on?'

'What do you mean, "What's going on"? I'm not a child. I just wanted a cigarette, that's all.'

'Cora,' and he speaks her name over several beats, elongated, an exasperated drawl. 'You agreed you'd stop, and at the very least you said you wouldn't smoke in the house near the children. You know all the research, you know what it does to their health, to all of us! Christ.' Cora looks at him – vigilant and decent, all clean. Good, so good.

'You're right, I'm sorry.' She steps across the hall and throws the remainder of the butt into the toilet.

'I'm worried about you. I wish you'd tell me what's wrong.'

'What do you mean? Nothing is wrong. I fancied a cigarette. You'll be late. You need to go.' She rubs her hand over her face, her fingertips moving the flesh over her bones.

'Darling, I'm not blind. You're not yourself, let me help. Talk to me.' He moves towards her. 'Please, Cora. God, you stink of fags. We'll talk tonight.' He turns his nose up at her and runs down the stairs, calling goodbye to his children.

'Daddy is cross with you.' The little boy emerges from his bedroom, his school uniform on.

'I know, and I'm cross with you, so we're all even. Go and eat some breakfast.'

Other people, so much better at this. At all of it. Talking, laughing, being wives, mothers, fathers; even dogs are more successful than her. She is a failure. She is driving carefully, each child strapped into the correct chair. She thinks about the moment when she'll be alone, and not required to answer their questions or chasten their squabbles. There is always thought, not speaking, not telling a soul. Just thinking. You can't punish a person for thoughts. She drops the boy off at school: she is late, with no make-up on and sloppily dressed. The other mothers all gather punctually, with their teeth brushed, hair washed and clothes carefully chosen. They even wear make-up. She imagines that they manage brisk but intense orgasms with their men. They stand around the school gate, and chat for another half an hour after their children have been absorbed by the building and the teachers.

How easy it is to the let the child go. And not think of him for those hours. And if something happens? It wasn't her fault, she entrusted him to professionals licensed by the government. She would be innocent, absolved.

They pull up outside a large building, and park the car between the painted lines on the tarmac. Just her and the girl. From the outside the building looks like a warehouse, somewhere industrial, where things are made and sold. A manufacturing plant where raw matter is processed into something new. She lifts the small girl out of the car and they walk hand in hand towards the large doors, the child excited and pulling against her grip. The reception is brightly lit and hints at the hygienic fun to come, all robust, colourful and wipe-clean. Cora hands over a card to the teenage boy at the desk.

'It's £10.50 for off-peak members, please. Dinky Dance class will start in fifteen minutes. Unfortunately the trampolines are closed today.' She hands him the cash, and at the green flash on the turnstile pushes her way into Kiddie Space, the anodyne fun palace her offspring crave.

A circle of women sit in amongst the primary brights; acidic textiles line the walls – corroding the fluid of the eye – rubber flooring cushions the precious little feet of their darlings. The women, heads together, discuss important items of existence, how to keep the future generation alive. This is not menial, this is crucial work, difficult and laborious and Cora is not up to the task. They talk and their children play noisily. There is no easy entrance into this esteemed coterie. Cora stands awkwardly, clinging to her daughter's hand, holding on to her badge of belonging, her safety. She takes shelter in the minute palm of her little girl, shielding herself from harm. The girl pulls away and runs through the circling women, oblivious to the danger. Cora spots a seat at a table and walks to it, her footsteps stupid and grateful. There's a scent of synthetic strawberries in the air they breathe. A pretence, mimicking the smell of innocent nature. She sits down, and takes out a magazine from her bag. Its pages slick as glass between her fingertips. She feels the heat of the woman sitting next to her, perhaps three feet away, breathing caution, her curly hair bouncing as she looks up every other minute or so to check on her child.

I should do that, I should check on my child too. Cora is capable of thinking something responsible. Her body is responsible. She looks up and peers through the miniature human bodies dashing about, until she spots hers in a pink dress. Her body mothers, all by itself, it produces without her will, without consent. It makes other humans and milk and mucus and shit. She is a disaster. A site of pure disaster, a mess. Her daughter runs past, a muddle of colour and dark hair, and climbs a ladder up into a padded orange cell that leads further on into ball-ponds, and down slides, and up more ladders. Cushioned everywhere by foam rubber if not mother-love these little precious treasures are cocky in their safety. Untouchable. Oblivious. Full little tummies toddle and swagger in their made-to-measure shoes. Damp fists clutch at fun, fun, fun.

The woman next to her catches her eye and smiles. 'Your little girl is a real live-wire isn't she?' Cora wonders how to respond, what might be the best answer. Mostly she hears parents complaining about their children with smug smiles etched onto their faces – their biology is a success. It lives and breathes! Triumph! What a little shit! What a beloved, bejewelled, little bastard! All that love, simple and easy. Look at us!!

'Yes, she's never still.'

'I can imagine. My boy – that's him in the green dungarees – is an absolute pain in the neck!' As the woman says this, the corners of her mouth are twitched up towards her ears, satisfied. 'He's almost four, but physically very developed. How old is your little one?'

'Four.' Cora looks down at the magazine on her lap, its surface reflecting light, fluid and calm. 'We've a son of six, but he's in school.'

A fresh yell joins in the cacophony. A new note to add to the leitmotif. Cora turns a page, revealing a different figure in a new pose.

'Isn't that your little girl crying?'

Cora scans the room. It's difficult to pick out one particular body in amongst all the others. The woman points to the climbing frame, at Jessica, her face deformed by tears.

'Yes. Yes it is.' She watches the child; it takes a breath, silent for a split second before screaming again. Perhaps she'll stop all by herself. The girl takes another breath, opening her mouth to continue the scream. 'I'll go over.' She stands and, unsure for a moment about whether to leave her bags or take them over with her, turns back to the woman, 'Would you mind watching my things?'

'No, no, of course not. Best get over there.'

As Cora jogs over to Jessica, she can feel the other women watching her, their eyes unblinking as they disapprove of her every move.

'What happened?' She picks the child up, its brittle limbs difficult to contain. 'Show me what hurts.'

The child sobs into her mother's chest, 'My head, I bumped my head. I want my Daddy.' She reaches her sticky hands up around her mother's neck, snorting snot and tears onto her t-shirt. 'It hurts, Mummy. It really hurts.' Cora's hand lifts and strokes the girl's head, gently, forwards then back, forwards then back, always the repetition, with the correct pressure and restraint. She experiences her own movement, her careful hand; she feels the hot body pressing into her, calming down, comforted. Her body mothers, with or without her consent.

Better, Jessica runs back to the danger. No one is watching Cora as she walks back, not even the woman sitting in the chair next to hers, guarding her things. She sits down. Her bags are there, untouched.

'Everything OK?'

'Yes, just a bump on the head. Nothing serious.'

'Luckily these places are well padded. I'm going to go up and get a tea. Fancy a cuppa?'

'No, thank you. I'm fine, thanks. But thank you.'

She is surrounded by happiness. She can make out their serenity behind their feigned exasperation. Like seeing heat rising on the horizon. They are haloed by it, coloured auras shimmer around them. Fat authors of these little characters. A garbled voice speaks over the tannoy, calling for a staff member. Cora wonders what it would be like to feel. She thinks about the fluid poured into her by her husband last night. How that fluid transforms: like all bodies of water, it shapes its surroundings whilst never remaining the same. His spunk changing her, filling her full of water, milk, blood, like a magic trick. It goes in as one thing and comes out another. Ta Da! Roll up, roll up and see the magic transforming liquid! She is nothing more substantial than a body of water.

When she first moved in with him, in love, she was nervous, intimidated. She was in her twenties, he was not much older, she had the bigger salary, he owned a flat. A flat filled with the past. He owned yellowed photographs of his ancestors, pieces of heavy, ugly furniture handed down through the family, a violin, crockery, silver cutlery with broken ivory handles, leather-bound books with gold lettering. She brought nothing from her family, no heirlooms, no idea what her ancestors looked like, beyond the vague references about her resemblance to her great-grandmother from an aunt who always spoke out of the corner of her mouth, as if she didn't want to be seen talking to Cora's sort.

He came from an aristocracy of care and forethought, an authentic family. Where quality and the practice of thinking about the future delineated them. Her family only ever existed in the present. Responding to their immediate needs: I want it now, I'm angry now, it's now, right now. Impulsive like animals, in debt and impoverished. That was the difference between them. Being able to imagine anything beyond now.

They met at work, both moving numbers around on screens, manipulating money. He pursued her, courted her with gifts, notes and flowers. They ate expensive dinners, sitting on fat, upholstered banquettes, and went on holidays together, walking in the Lake District or swimming in the transparent Mediterranean. Everything as it should be. Precise, proper and in the correct order. He was the perfect man. Moving in with him was the logical next step. It was the right thing to do. And she loved him.

He was good at loving, practised at it. She'd had practice too, had been in love or something like it before, but he had lived with someone else and had even considered marriage. She moved into his flat because it made sense, why incur the expense of moving, he said. She didn't like to tell him that his ex haunted every room.

One day, not long after moving in, she decided to clear up the kitchen. A basket full of paperwork, old bills and catalogues took up too much space on the counter. It was untidy, and didn't fit in with her idea of their shared home. She began sorting and sifting through, creating small piles of paper carefully classified according to which company they were from, and what was outstanding. She was diligent and hardworking. She took her responsibility seriously. In amongst all the paper she found a notebook, a simple unadorned notebook. She flipped it open. The first page revealed nothing more interesting than a list of food to be ordered from the Indian take-away. She thumbed through, revealing more lists: to-do lists, shopping lists, things to pay, things to forget. Random phone numbers. Birthday dates. Nothing sinister. All written before her presence in his life. When she was loving someone else. History. And then, feeling warmly towards him, smiling to herself at his charming attempts at organisation, she looked more closely at a To Do list. On Sunday the 18th of November, eighteen months before they'd met, he was to: take tea in bed to his Beloved and Moby; slip her a length; do a small tidy up; phone parents; wash gym kit; slip Lucy another length! (his exclamation mark), make beloved Lucy a roast dinner. She turned another page, and then another. A Christmas list. With both their names, and the names of their families and friends. Theirs. Their little silly cute life all punctuated and listed on paper.

Cora's stomach leaked bile into her throat. Her head throbbed. Stupid to look, stupid. Her fault for prying; ignorance is always better. See what you get for knowing! Only pain. A dirty pain. Better to not know, only to believe. She deserved to feel this agony. Who was she to rummage in his things, in his flat, where she was a guest? She hated him. How dare he? How dare he be playful and loving with someone else? How could he have desired someone else? He could have, should have cleaned the evidence out. Revised his past. Who was Moby? Did they have a threesome? Was it a friend? He called her his Beloved. She wasn't the only one. She waited for him to come back. He was out with work colleagues, trustworthy him. Who'd never cheated on a woman, ever, and certainly wouldn't now. Or so he always said. She walked to the window, and looked up the street in the direction of the station. Looking for his walk, his shape pressed out in black in the streetlamp dark. A little drunk possibly. She sat back down.

When he came in, tired, happy to see her, kissing her, she turned her back. It hurt even to say it.

'Who is Moby?' She'd have liked to say this calmly, but her voice wavered, like an animal's cry. It wasn't a human voice. Betraying too much without requiring words. She blushed.

'What? I don't know.' He slumped onto the sofa, his back curved like a shell. 'You took Lucy and Moby tea in bed. Who was Moby?'

'Cora! What are you talking about?'

She picked up the notebook and held it up to him. He laughed. Read his list.

'Moby was her cuddly penguin. A stuffed toy! She cuddled him in bed.'

'What? A toy?! How pathetic! A grown woman with a cuddly toy. Oh my God! What an idiot. That's fucking pathetic.' Her hands were numb and her chest hurt. Her body seemed to constrict, to pull itself tight around her, protecting, ready to run, making the separation between them, the growing distance even bigger. She wanted him to prove he loved her, Cora. Loved her more than the other one, the perfect, tennis playing, toy-cuddling one. She wanted to undo herself and fuse into him. But he just stood there, opposite her, completely distinct.

'Alright, Cora. What do you want me to say? So she's an idiot. That was then, a long time ago. Why are you freaking out?'

'And did you 'slip it to her' twice in one day?'

'I don't remember. Probably not. She didn't like sex much, besides she'd started seeing the bloke behind my back by then. Why are we even talking about this? Christ, Cora it's in the past.'

Cora wanted to stop then. Not to feel angry, or jealous, or hurt. She was embarrassed by her behaviour. She wanted to go to bed with him. To forget what she had seen. She wanted to eradicate Lucy, pretty Lucy, clever, tennis playing Lucy, Lucy who could cook, ski and sing, and play Poker, and get on with his mother, Lucy. Adult Lucy, who cuddled toy penguins in bed and gave them names.

'Do you love me as much as you loved her?

'What a question! I'm not with her am I? Lucy left me, she cheated on me, you know the story. Whatever was there was destroyed. We moved on, she's with someone else, I'm with you, surely that says everything? Isn't that proof enough?'

'So does that mean you're only with me because she left you?'

'Jesus, Cora, please. Leave it alone. I love you.'

Not long after the incident he asked her to marry him, and had remained loving and loyal. But she flinched when he called her his Beloved, or wrote lists that said things like: buy bread and milk; pay credit card; kiss my Beloved; clean the oven. Because she was just another one pressed to fit into a Beloved-shaped hole in his life.

'Mummy!' Jessica stands in front of her, a still body amidst all the hurtling children. 'I want a drink please.' The little girl places her fat little hand on her mother's. Cora leans back, into the rigid plastic seat and looks at the girl.

'What would you like to drink?'

'Beena, please.'

'Ribena. Say Ribena. You're not a baby anymore. OK?'

'OK, Mummy.'

Cora looks at her daughter, her flesh, her spit, her blood; an outcome, a transformed fluid. Shape shifter. I am blank. She feels herself recede, hears her own breath, tidal – in and out, sucked in through the mouth, is conscious of the small child's eyes watching her, the black eyelashes clicking open and shut, she is looking at something dreadful and complex. A hollow opens in her middle, a gap; she tries to fill it with air and takes a deep breath in. It fills with nothing. A network of veins on the child's wrist is theatrical in the bright light. Cora stands, Jessica's dark head reaches to her waist, she is a bird, brittle-boned, vulnerable, flightless. 'Let's just go home.' The child starts to cry, huge gulping sobs, her small fist rubbing at her eyes.

'I want to stay,' she whines, kicking and flailing as Cora picks her up. The other mothers watch her as she leaves.

The child is sleeping. Flat on her back, her hair slicked with sweat, she sighs, her forbidden thumb close to her mouth. At the doorway to her room, Cora watches. I should love you. I should love you. The child is tucked into her pink room; the curtains at the window ebb and flow with the breeze, reshaping, remade with the current. The house is quiet, naptime, scheduled peace, time for Mummy to relax, when the child-rearing manual instructs Cora to 'flick through a magazine or watch some TV'. She is absolutely NOT to attempt to catch up on household chores, this is counter-productive, she must value herself and allow herself to enjoy some ME time. She could make herself a cup of coffee even, what a treat!

Cora stands in the doorway, not leaning against the frame, she stands squarely on both feet, her hands trail by her sides. She is unnatural, this pose is unnatural, but she stands there like that in order to trace a vague ailment. Indistinct, she can only distinguish between her body and the outside world if she concentrates on each limb, narrowing down her search to inch-by-inch compartments of flesh. She is unfeeling, it takes time to locate the area that troubles her. She turns and walks into her room. She removes her clothes, carefully removing each item and folding them into logical shapes. There is a full-length mirror on the wardrobe door: it is to be avoided usually, but today she confronts it, to search for the problem.

Looking at herself, naked. Reflected back, she receives herself. It's said that one is composed only of memories, and yet her body speaks for itself, her stretch marks, scars, freckles, fading tan-lines. Large raised moles, one with a hair to pluck out regularly along with other hair removal. The thick scar where her daughter was cut from her body. Her belly hangs like fabric over the seam, loosely draped. Too disgusting to revel in. She could be read, as one would read a book. The body belongs first to the species before it belongs to her. But then it doesn't belong to her, she doesn't possess it. She can't give it away. Neither can anyone take it. Not yet anyway, not until it becomes truly just a body, when she's dead. It is her intermediary, SHE is only what she looks at, thinks about, says. That's all she is. She is only ever happening, now, immediate, never recognisable to herself, always changing, only ever in the present tense. And tucked away inside her flesh is the secret of her eventual death, hers alone, the death that she will never know, because she will not be able to talk about it, or think it. When the body finally becomes just a body, only others will be able to own it, move it, rob from it. Indecent, humiliated, free floating, without meaning, innocent and incapable.

But she isn't alive, she knows this absolutely. She craves sensation, to pull her back into the land of the living. Isn't that what they say when you are there and yet not there? When you are startled from a daydream? Welcome back to the Land of the Living? Looking at herself, the body, female, all present and correct. Her husband likes to kiss her all over, tenderly, licking her skin; he expects this to be pleasurable to her. The female body is in luck with its multiple pleasure zones, its vigour and vim, its insatiability, with its capacity for multiple orgasms, not limited to one measly climax. Always ready. Lady Luck.

Raising her hand to her face, she pulls open her eyes as wide as the lids will stretch, letting in as much light as possible. She is a medium through which light, sound, information passes. She read once that Newton had removed his own eye from its socket without causing injury, using a bodkin. The body will graciously allow all kinds of experiments, and can mend all kinds of wounds if given time. She wonders if his experiment had hurt, or changed the way his eye behaved once firmly back in his head. She ran her hand down over her neck, toward her breast. This should feel good. Should be arousing. It isn't. She experiences the pressure of her hand on her skin, she senses that there is touch, but she feels nothing. She circles her nipple with the tip of her finger, it responds, as it should, protruding. Everything her body does – she does – is in response, well-mannered, well-choreographed, a set piece. Inauthentic, not a real response, she doesn't answer, not for herself, she parrots the expected reply. Her nipple hardens to touch, to kisses, to suckling. She feels nothing. She is a monster, a repetition of well-rehearsed gestures.

Digging in her nails, she pinches the nipple, twisting it like a dial. There is a flicker of life. She breathes, her eyelids twitch. She chastises, punishes her body for its lack. Because it fails every expectation. Finally, she has had enough. She is enraged. In the room next to hers, the child sleeps, unaware of her mother who is not enough. Who will never be enough. Cora pinches and twists harder. The peak of her nipple is white, entirely bloodless, purified. Sensation cuts through, like a dagger through thick drapery, alive. She suffers, and it isn't enough. She cannot pinch hard enough. She fails.

Cora wraps her bathrobe around her, the red towelling harsh against her half alive skin. She runs down the stairs, past the sleeping child, into the kitchen. She opens drawers and cupboards, looking for an instrument to help her. She doesn't want knives, isn't interested in cutting and slicing, in doubling herself, that would be disastrous.

There is the washing line. Outside and dangerous. No clothes hang from it; it isn't a washday. But the pegs, all lined up like birds, grip the line tightly. Cheap plastic pincers, the pressure applied by a coil of wire, closed shut. Innocent, they have no choice but to act according to their design. Until they are broken, they will pinch together, crushing what comes between. Merciless.

Barefoot, Cora runs across the grass to the line and takes two. She isn't afraid. She feels light, and giddy. She is as excited as a drunk. She runs back across the kitchen and up the stairs. Back in the muted light of the bedroom, she watches herself, watches the fingers of one hand compress flat the bulk of her breast, forcing the nipple forward as the fingers on the other hand grip the two ends of the clothes peg. She fits the nipple into the gape of the pincers as far as she can, and lets go of the peg. It snaps shut. She silences herself and refuses to groan. Taking the other breast she feeds it to the grabbing peg. She is brand new. The surprise of the pain transforms her. She is alive. There is no blood, no filth. Only purity. She is punished and in pain. Her breathing shallow and ecstatic.

Everything moves apart, everything. I listened to a radio programme in the car about dark matter and the universe. The universe is expanding, the planets and stars are moving further and further away from each other, and the gaps, these ever increasing spaces are filled with dark matter. It's inevitable I suppose. Perhaps that's what this is, the gap between us is filling with dark matter, dark matter that pushes us further and further apart. Perhaps it's inevitable.

I took you to meet my parents, much sooner than you took me to meet yours. I wanted to show you off, I was so proud of you. This clever, sexy woman who wanted to spend her time with me. You've always said that I cared too much about their opinion, that it's odd to be so close to my family. But it's not like that, at least not as simple as you make out. Of course I wanted them to like you and for you to like them, but just because that made life a bit easier. Their opinion wouldn't have caused me to change my mind or anything; I'm not a total sap. God, what a business it all is, this family stuff. But truth be told, I enjoy it, I enjoy belonging to you and the kids, to my parents, to my sister. I'm proud to be uncle, brother, son, husband and father. It doesn't matter how difficult it is sometimes. Perhaps that does make me a sentimental fool. But it matters, it matters to me and it should matter to you.

We arrived in time for lunch. It was summer and you were wearing a strappy dress that floated around your ankles and green plastic flip-flops. I remember them so clearly. Green plastic flip-flops and bright pink painted toenails. Your hair was scraped up into a ponytail. The sun picked up the red glints in the brown strands. You wore a bronze bangle on your right wrist that I'd bought for you from Brixton market and that you wore all the time. It was the first piece of jewellery that I'd ever bought you. It was cheap, junk really, but it looked good against your skin and you liked it. I wonder where it is now, lost in one of our various flat and house moves. All the different places we've lived in, that define us and our history together. You never wear jewellery anymore, except your wedding ring, of course.

It was a glorious day, as they always seem to be in retrospect. But it was a lovely day. Warm and sunny and clear. I should've prepared you more, I think now. But at the time I thought you were so marvellous that I couldn't imagine any situation you couldn't take in your stride and I couldn't bear to say anything that would hurt you or diminish you in any way. What would you have thought if I'd started telling you what to wear or not to smoke or any of those stupid things? It really shouldn't matter what anyone thinks anyway. I suppose that kind of hurt, that pretending to be helpful and offering constructive feedback, but really just being spiteful and demeaning, comes later in a relationship. When you're more comfortable, when you feel able to take out your vague, petty anger on your partner.

We stood at the door and knocked. The sunlight was rushing in behind you and it was so bright it almost erased you, blanked you out rather than revealed you. I can't explain it. You disappeared for a moment in the bright sun.

You'd said nothing as we'd driven up the drive and parked. The house sitting there. Its neat 1930s suburban satisfaction, double-fronted, squat and square with that huge garden. I didn't think all that then of course. I didn't think. It was just home. On that short drive out of town into the commuter belt, you sang along to the CD player and smiled at me, your skirt hitched up around your thighs and your feet propped up on the dashboard. You couldn't believe how green and leafy it was still being so close to London and you laughed and said, 'All the houses are alike. Big and detached but still alike, still like being on a housing estate. Just with gravel drives and swimming pools.' I didn't know how to answer that except to retort that our pool was only tiny. I understood then that somehow we hadn't lived up to your expectations, you were disappointed in me, but I didn't think it was serious, I didn't think it would matter.

My mother opened the front door, her blonde hair cut to her shoulders, dressed in shorts and a polo shirt, the two spaniels at her feet. She opened the door wide and smiled at us both. She liked you on sight, I could tell. She even hugged you. She walked ahead, leading us and the dogs through the house, asking questions about our journey and the traffic. You walked beside me, looking straight ahead, dead ahead; even when I squeezed your hand, you didn't look up at me. God, we were both so nervous. Dad was waiting for us in the garden, past the terrace, which Mother had laid for lunch, over the lawn and past the stand of cypress trees that Sally and I had hidden behind as children, to the small terrace by the pool. You hated it on sight. You've never said it outright, but I know you thought we were pretentious snobs, it was written all over your face. But it was just home and our house wasn't as big as some of our neighbours... Christ, silly that I try to justify it now.

Anyway, we followed Mum, and Dad stood up and walked towards us, his arms wide and welcoming. He's always been so good at that, disarming people, immediately warm and kind. 'Well, look at the lovebirds!' I loved that, though I was embarrassed too. I loved that he could see how much I adored you. We sat down on the wicker chairs and he poured us a glass of Pimms each from the jug on the table. We sat side by side and I held your hand. I watched you chatting with them, answering their questions, being utterly charming, managing to dodge Mum's inevitable invitation to play tennis sometime. You seemed comfortable, though you sounded different with a new accent. Best behaviour I suppose. You know everything I've ever done since then has been for you. I think you should know that.

Mother rounded us up in her usual way, what you now call bossy and shrill but I just think of as organised, and ushered us towards lunch. She sat us opposite each other, facing across the table, almost as if she wanted to separate us and have you all to herself. Divide and conquer you'd said later, but you're a cynic where mother's concerned, she just wanted the chance to chat to you, to get to know you. We're a close family, we look out for one another and if you're special to one of us then the rest want to get to know you too. That's all it is. You have to remember how much she'd loved Lucy. It can't have been easy for her when Lucy left. It was a loss for all the family. They were upset for me, but upset for themselves too.

You sat there, looking small and dark next to her, as she divvied up the quiche and the potatoes, passing the salad bowl and the dressing like she always has, like she's the expert, in charge. As she always said, Father might be the boss at work but she's the head of the household. You sat across from me, your brown eyes hidden by the vase of brightly coloured flowers that mother had put in the middle of the table like a screen. And then handing the bread round, Dad asked you what your father did for a living. Just like that, not like it mattered, like we were in the middle ages or something, he was just being polite. You smiled and said 'my dad's in retail.' Which was sort of true, I suppose, it was only when I met him that I found out he sold used cars. It didn't matter; I can't imagine why you'd think it would. You didn't elaborate and the conversation moved to our work, and the weather and our holiday plans. Safe territory, firm ground.

You don't much like your own parents, at least that's how it seems and I've never understood that. They're perfectly alright. Especially your dad. Your mother is so quiet it's like she's not even in the room, but your dad has real substance, he's interested in the world around him at least and they both love the children, and the kids adore them – you can't fault them for that. But you seem to have no interest in them, no warmth and I wonder why?

We sat there drinking wine and eating and you said all the right things and complimented the food and made them both laugh with your clever jokes and then Sally arrived with David. Sally with her ways and means. I'm not blind to her flaws. Really I'm not. I know she was an idiot with her pinched looks and she *didn't need to mention running into Lucy at the club, but that's just the way she's always been. She can be a little bit bitchy, but it's only because she's protective of me. It's funny; you have to laugh at her. To see it for what it is – a sister looking out for her brother. To be honest, I'd be the same I suppose, in her shoes. She didn't know you from Adam, and she didn't want us all to be hurt again. You'll admit things are better now between you both, she's been very supportive since we had the kids, I know that she's a bit sniffy that you've gone back to work; especially as she's so happy to stay at home. But it should be left at that. Horses for courses. She's so good with the kids and she offers to help all the time. She's even offered to have the kids for us so that we can have a weekend away together.*

After lunch mother suggested we take the dogs for a walk in the woods but she took one look at your flip flops and said something like, 'They just won't do. You can't go for a walk in those. What silly shoes, whatever made you wear beach shoes for lunch? Never mind...what size are you? Perhaps we can lend you something.' Your tiny little feet, no match for my sister and mother's size sevens. I know how that must have sounded, but she didn't mean to offend, that's just the way she is. Dad and Sally didn't even notice. It's just the way she is. Mother is very blunt and honest. You slipped off to the loo and it seemed like you were gone for ages and when you got back you looked upset, your cheeks pink as if they'd been pinched. You never told me why. Though I guessed, of course. There were no shoes she could lend you. We never went for that walk.

You've not really given them a chance since then, though they're charming to you and I know you're civil, but it's not really as I would hope and both my parents adore you. They've told me so, several times. It would make me happy if you got along with them. It really would. I can't see that it's too much to ask. Anyway, there we are. That's how it is. After that first lunch with them, we drove back to my flat in silence. Except when you said 'I wish you'd told me how wealthy your family is' and I couldn't think of anything to say back. And that's my problem; it's only after the event that I can think of a reasonable response. At the time I'm usually too caught up in the moment to think of how best to answer you. I'm not good with conflict. But they aren't wealthy; alright, they're comfortable, but Dad has worked hard, and Mum too. They're not the stuck up arses that you seem to think. Sally and I weren't spoilt, we had to work for things, it wasn't all handed to us on a plate. We are not unusual. We are ordinary, all of us, there is nothing special about any one of us. We are ordinary, normal people who do ordinary, normal things. And that should be a comfort. At least it is to me.

He opens the front door to them. A light is on in the porch; it is a welcome, a friendly beckoning. A custom. The light is a machine that produces this meaning: 'Come on in, our house is open and warm! We are safe, you are safe. Everything is just right.' Everyone knows this. The light is also about security, and banishing any dark refuge for danger. It allows for the scrutiny of all visitors. But this is not discussed. It is not the custom to talk openly about danger. In fact it is considered rude to identify and confront any threat until it reveals itself absolutely. It's more polite to wait until an actual incident has occurred.

He opens the door to them and steps aside, he smiles, they enter, wiping their feet.

'Grandma! Granddad!' Patrick and Jessica run into the hall from the sitting room where they have been watching a cartoon. Stepping closer, they are lost in their grandparents' embrace. Hugged and tugged, they giggle and clamour for sweeties and treats, for presents that declare and entreat for undying love.

'What's Grandma got in her bag?' the older woman teases, half opening the rim of her black leather handbag. The children hop from foot to foot, trance-like, they dance around her, worshippers in an ecstatic rite. 'Please, Grandma! Please!' They perform circles around her as she laughs and removes her overcoat, helped at once by a clash of gallantry from both her husband and her son-in-law. Their hands entangle politely, they make a mess of the thing. Neither manages to catch the coat as it falls to the floor.

'Careful! That wasn't cheap, that.' The older man picks the coat up from the tiled floor and slaps out non-existent dust and grime as if the coat were choking and he were dislodging an obstruction from its throat.

'Too many cooks! No harm done. Come on Jess, Patch, see what I've got.' The older woman hands the children two large

69

bags of jelly sweets in carnival colours. Far too bright for nature, they are reminiscent of the colours medieval artists painted their visions of heaven and hell. Hyper real, godly, nothing as prosaic as nature would be good enough for the children. In fact children must be shielded from reality at all times. To Cora, standing at the kitchen door, her offspring's sugary desire is obscene.

'There you are! We wondered where you'd got to.'

'Hello Dad, Mum. You alright? Not before dinner you two, put the sweets away now.' She makes a small stand, in front of them all. She is, after all, the mother, the authority.

'Ah! Don't be a spoilsport, Cora. They don't get to see us very often, do they? Let them have a little treat.'

The husband looks over the heads of his parents-in-law at Cora, his eyes widening in warning. A marital semaphore, that guides and protects, he then winks at her, signalling that he is ON HER SIDE. She obeys and lets the subject drop. She must accept a higher authority. She must keep the peace.

'Come on, let's go through to the sitting room, we can get comfortable till dinner's ready. What can I get you to drink?' He manages them, as he manages all people, with ease. She envies him this. They all follow her husband into the room. He switches off the television. The children know better than to moan, having already been briefed on the etiquette of having visitors, even if those visitors were Grandma and Granddad. The older couple sit together on the sofa. Pulling the children onto their laps, they barely glance at the other two adults in the room.

'Same as always. I'll have a scotch and water please. Mary, you'll have your usual?' The woman looks up from her game with Jessica and nods. 'And a wine for Mary please.'

Cora turns from the room with her husband.

'I'll check on dinner.'

When Cora comes back into the room the tableau has changed. Someone has drawn the curtains closed and the children are now sitting on the floor, sweets by their side, opening boxes, more new toys. The adults each nurse a glass in their right hand. There's music playing in the background, something unknown to her. Her mother is watching the children tearing at the packaging around their new plastic treasure, their little fingers curved like hooks, resembling utensils, not sensitive flesh. Her father leans towards her husband, speaking only to him; they both laugh, her husband turning the laugh in her direction. He winks at her. Everything that happens, happens between words. Her father stands and walks towards her, stepping over the cardboard mess surrounding the children and puts his arm around her. 'Got a hug for your old man?'

'Of course!' She steps into his mass and leans her head against his shoulder. He is proud of me. Proud of her. Good husband, good children, house, job, car. Tick, tick, tick. All complete, a satisfactory result. He feels reassured. She steps back, out of him. We can't belong together anymore, Daddy. The children and husband have come between us, they separate us with their demands. She looks at his face, in close up it disintegrates, fragments and becomes unrecognisable. If only the eye had the sophistication of a camera lens, eternally disinterested. A large raised mole, flesh-coloured, grows in the corner of his nose. His eyes droop underneath long eyebrows. His mouth is moist and exposed. He looks back at her, and reassembles as she watches. He is her father again. Her protector.

'Dinner's ready.'

They are kind and good. A contract of flesh and thought exists in the gathering of atoms, the accumulation that makes up this family. They try. They try to love and manage it. They take their shapes because of the spaces that interrupt. They are good humans, suppressing all that is animal. They are good. But Cora is a beast, fragile and violent. Compulsive.

'We're all animals. Nothing more, nothing less.'

'Cora! You're a strange girl! What an interruption!' They all laugh. What a joke! What wit she has. Even the children join in, chuckling at what they don't understand, learning the script, repeating it over and over. Mummy is so very funny!

They sit around the table in the kitchen. She sits at the head, closest to the oven. A large blue casserole dish is in the centre of the table, filled with beef stew and dumplings. Because I am human, I am rotten. If I didn't intervene, just remained animal I would succeed. Cora is human, she thinks, she is thinking, she has thoughts. The body succeeds. Stop thinking. She hands a large metal spoon to her mother.

'Why don't you serve us all.' Her mother takes the spoon, and stands up.

'So, I meant to say as well, that they are really good people. I'm looking forward to working with them.' Cora's husband hands his plate to his mother-in-law who fills it.

'Come on, pass me your plates. Let's eat.' Cora's mother turns to her. 'This smells delicious, Darling. Really good.'

'Will you earn a percentage from the deal? What's your reward for all the work?' The older man leans forward on his elbows, his hands folded into a large fist.

'John, pass me your plate, please dear.' He passes his wife his plate. She fills it with the slop of meat and vegetables. Cooked for so long the ingredients have begun to lose form. Already the process of assimilation is beginning. Rendered to pure matter. Excrement is holy.

'Thanks, love.' He loves his wife, his daughter, her husband and children. This is a statement of fact. It just is, no thought, nor critique. He begins to eat. 'Very good. Almost as good as your mother's!'

They laugh. They are in no hurry. They eat. Her husband pours more wine. The children chatter and laugh together. The adults pay them all due attention. Cora watches. They have never been hungry. They are privileged children. Fed regularly and with diligent consideration of nutrients and trans fats, cholesterol and salt. Perhaps fierce mother-love is ignited when your children are starving? When they cling to you, bug-eyed, bellies distended and hollow. Maybe then love abounds. The scrape and shriek of metal on china punctuates the conversation as they eat every morsel on their plates. They will want more, they always want more. Their teeth clack and grind as they chew the fibres of the meat. The mouths curl and pose. Eating and speaking. The jaws gyrate in the skull. The mouths hunger and hunger. Their bellies are crammed with meat.

'What are you doing for Cora's birthday?' Mary looks towards her son-in-law. Her glass in hand, empty.

'Not sure are we?' he glances towards Cora but his eyes miss her, avoid her. 'I wanted to take her away somewhere. Perhaps a spa or something. Lots of pampering and lazing around. Both of us could do with a rest. A weekend break with nothing to do but eat and be fussed over, you know, a massage and all that. But Cora doesn't like that sort of thing, do you?'

'No, she never has, have you, dear? Never been a proper girl. Never been one for make-up and manicures. Difficult to buy for really, can't just get her a bottle of perfume or a facial for a gift.'

'Not like her mother! You can't go wrong buying you a vat of face cream and a shop full of dresses. Isn't that right?' He chuckles, he is right, always right.

'Well you should do something special. Not just let it go. You need to celebrate.' Mary reaches for the wine bottle and fills her glass. 'I've no idea what we'll get you, Cora.'

'I don't want a gift. Honestly, I'm not bothered by birthdays. It hardly seems to matter. Seems silly to spend all that money.' The children are quiet, listening to the strange conversation that lingers in air like smoke.

'Hard to believe you're my daughter sometimes!' the older woman laughs 'How you came from my body I can't imagine! You've said that before, haven't you John?'

'I have indeed said that. Well. You'll work it out between you. Perhaps we should just get her vouchers, Mary. What do you say, you could get something for the kids?'

'Let's get mummy a guinea pig! We could all love that.' Patrick grins at his ingenuity.

'Yes! Please mummy, please?' Jessica bounces on her chair.

'No, that's not a good idea,' Cora says; her hands tingle and prickle.

'Oh, why not?' her father asks before picking at a piece of meat stuck between his teeth.

Cora looks at her husband, he shrugs his shoulders, smiling. It's her decision.

'Because it's too much responsibility for kids, that's why.'

'Mummy had a rabbit, Kids. Didn't you, Cora?'

'Yes, mum. I did. Don't you remember what happened?'

'What do you mean?'

'It died, mum. I forgot to feed it. You went in the shed and found it, remember? Dead in its hutch.'

'No, that's not what happened. Is it?' The woman looks at her husband who shakes his head. The children are silent, watching the adults. Jessica chews on the ends of her hair, splitting the strands. Patrick rubs at his ear. Cora looks down at her hands.

She is once again separated from her flesh – the only thing that can be touched- she is distanced from herself. In her bra, tucked safely away are her perfect new bruises. But they've stopped throbbing; the source of the joy is exhausted and needs stoking up. Her husband gets up from the table and begins to gather up the plates, the knives and forks. The meal is over, the children tired and full. The atmospheric pressure is huge, crushing.

'Shall we go and read a story before bedtime?' Mary stands, her weight evenly distributed over her two feet. Just as her love is evenly distributed between the children. She carries her bulky load well, and never lets its tip to one side. She takes the children by the hand and leads them out of the door towards the stairs. All happily wrapped up in clichés. 'Better say goodnight to Mummy. Go and give her a kiss.' They walk over and put their arms around Cora. Patrick's head level with her chest. She holds them, pressing them as hard as she can against herself. Wanting to feel them. It is as if she is holding a container full of mercury, hazardous and difficult to control, requiring a firm hand. She is untouched by the small declarations of hands and compressed lips. Love is a violence that wreaks havoc on the health. It demands a dark sacrifice. The children wriggle against her pressure.

'Mummy you're hurting me.' She releases them, immediately. They are entirely safe.

Sitting alone, the sofa's soft cushions an affront to her body's secret demand, she takes off her shoes. Her head tips back. Upstairs she can hear the muffled sounds of a song being sung and the repeated 'Night, Nights' from the children. Her mother putting them to bed. Lullabies and story telling, the intricate skill of sending them off to sleep. It can't be taught, it is innate; it is everything Cora lacks. Her husband and father are still in the kitchen, cleaning up and talking. They are comfortable in this house. They are aware of the limits of their position, the responsibilities and rewards. The pleasure that is available to them. They are humans that think and remember. She is only instinct. That is the problem. The urge to hurt and its recurrence. On/ off, on/off, on/off. Dead again. There is no respite from her mortality. This dead skin draped over a dead body. She allows her hands to lapse into useless lumps on her knees. The memory of being alive again, earlier in the day, disturbs her corpse. She was resurrected, and then dead again.

Mary enters the room, smiling and perfumed. Well turned out, she's a woman who prizes cleanliness and self-respect. She was never a beauty, but ensured that she was a wife her husband could be proud of. Hair and make-up immaculate before she left the house, dressed always in smart clothing, nothing brash, nothing showy. The house comfortable, the child – they weren't blessed with the joy of a large family – Cora, always well-mannered, polite and clean. She never bought ready-made meals, always shopped carefully to stretch the household budget.

She is capable, with the capacity to contain a family's worth of spite and disappointments locked safely away inside her. It'll all be buried with her, securely disposed of out of harm's way.

She sits next to Cora on the sofa, sinking into the lenient cushions. 'Well, that's them off to bed.'

'Yes. You're so good with them. They love having you here.'

'It's easy with such lovely little ones. They're absolute darlings.'

'Yes. I suppose it is. I'm lucky. Was I easy to look after when I was a child?' Cora shifts and turns her body so that she can look at her mother.

'Oh, you were no trouble. No trouble at all. I just wish you'd had a brother or sister. Still, it wasn't meant to be, we were lucky to have you at least.' Mary raises her hand to her face, and pushes a grey curl back from her forehead.

'Did you ever wish things had been different? That you'd stayed single maybe? Had a career instead of marrying Dad?' Cora begins to pick at the skin around her fingernails, tearing at the flesh.

'No, not really. I feel very grateful for my blessings.' Mary takes a deep breath.

'Really? You've never wondered what life would be like if you'd made different choices? If you'd not married, not had me?'

Mary looks at her. Cora feels her eyes testing, searching for signs of health, of decay, of sickness. 'No, I don't ever think that. If I thought like that it would be like wishing you dead, like murdering you with my own hands. It's a terrible thing to even think of.' She sighs, her body lifting then drooping with the breath.

The house shakes a little as a car speeds past. 'Don't pick your nails, dear. I thought you'd outgrown that habit.' She pats Cora's hand.

Cora wants her mother to reach out and caress her head, to feel the cool pressure of the fingers. She remembers the touch of her mother's hand better than she remembers anything else about Mary. She reaches forward and takes her mother's hand, stroking it, and laying her own out next to it. Side by side, the two hands flattened out for examination.

'They're so different. I always thought my hands would be like yours.'

'No! Yours are lovely and elegant, not like my little paws.'

'I'd always recognise your hands, they never seem to change, no matter what. Funny you call them paws, when our hands are what separate us from animals, if you think about it. Having hands to use tools is what makes us human.'

'Well, I don't know, what about monkeys? Don't they have hands? I always thought mine looked like those little squirrel paws. You should make the most of your pretty ones, paint your nails or something nice like that.'

She takes her hand from her daughter and lays it in her lap as if it is an object removed from her body. It is just after eight o'clock. Cora places her own hand on the sofa. She wants to rearrange her body, place it in a different posture, but doesn't want to disturb her mother. Her body, a body once carried inside her mother's, now revolts against her, constructing a mutiny. They sit together, in a space that seems to shrink around them, closing in and dividing them from the rest of the house. Mary stands, pushing at the sofa and shifting forwards to hoist herself up. 'I'll see what the men are up to, shall I?'

Cora nods, she is an amateur, unable to think of the right thing to say or do. 'Shall I bring you a drink? A tea perhaps and some biscuits?' Cora can't think of any other answer except to say yes, as she has always done to her mother's offers of food and drink. She'll let herself be fattened like a Christmas pig.

She looks out of the window at the street. Outside is an invitation. The evening beckons to her, out in the street, all that light; from the yellow bulbs in the houses, from television shows that pulse beams of colour, the downcast glow of the streetlamp, so much light that the stars fade and are just rumours of a presence. People hurry in and hurry out of their homes. Cora sits as still as she can, as any kind of movement would be an acceptance of the kind invite. And then what would happen? Just about anything that she could imagine. But with all the limits imposed by reality. There would be no remaking of a life, no clean cut, no clean sweep, only dirt and shame. What sort of a mother leaves her children? What sort of a person just runs away from their family? What sort of a mother gives birth? What kindness is that, birthing a thing only for it to die? Mary enters the room carrying a plate of carefully arranged chocolate biscuits and a cup of tea and the light turns. The invitation is declined.

You were always so jealous and insecure. It was quite flattering. I liked it at first. I liked that you loved me enough to care about my past. It was a good feeling, you being spiky and possessive. You wanted to know all the gory details about Lucy and the other women I'd been with. As if me telling you the truth would dispel your fears. I guess it's like how I torture myself now with images of you being intimate with someone else. Someone else's hands on your body. I've never felt like this before. In the beginning when you were jealous and scared, I was completely comfortable and at ease. I trusted you and I trusted our love for one another. That you had loved before didn't matter, if anything it was reassuring that you had a past, that you'd been with other men. It meant you'd satisfied your curiosity, and I suppose I felt lucky that you'd chosen me, that out of all those others, it was me you wanted. But now, fuck; I'm terrified you're seeing someone else. Everything has changed. I'm not confident about us, or your feelings for me anymore. Now I'm jealous.

In the beginning it was you with the green-eyed monster. Nothing I said seemed to console you. No matter that it was you I wanted to marry, you I wanted to be with, you just fixated on my past. You compared yourself all the time, your body, your sexual technique. You asked strange questions that had the odd effect of making me think about the very thing you didn't want me to think about... You'd ask what her body was like and so I'd picture her in order to describe her to you and reassure you. It seemed perverse to me, for you to insist on discussing her in a way that made her wholly present to me, when I was quite happy to forget her, to leave her in my past. It began to wear on me eventually. I got tired of the insecurity. It was all so long ago.

Having sex with Lucy was like having sex with an actress. It was so unreal. All image. She made perfect faces, not dirty porno style, but you know, art house erotic, pouting and eyes closed, supposedly sexy but totally fake. I used to feel that if I just stopped and stood back she would continue the performance and sounds on her own like an automaton. At times it felt that her gasps and sighs were oddly out of sync with what was actually going on. She insisted on bathing just before, so she never smelt of anything but perfume and deodorant. Her hair all perfectly blow-dried and her face made up with lipstick. She dressed in stockings and elaborate lingerie, all of which is supposed to be a man's ultimate fantasy I know, but it was off-putting, a mask; sex with her had to be prettied up, tidy and premeditated. All the make-up and costumes were less an invitation and more a warning not to touch her or mess up the effect with my brutish sex drive. Look but don't touch.

I much prefer us, or at least the way we used to be. Imperfect, snaggle-toothed, hairy, smelly and totally real and totally beautiful. Normal. I've always loved the way you smell, your natural untouched scent, dark and female. And though you're insecure about how you look now, I love how your body has resolutely and inexorably come to represent the history of us. Your body is like a diagram describing our lives together, our family, your body is a map of us. Surely that can only ever be beautiful?

I've never missed Lucy. Contrary to your fears. When she moved out all I felt was relief. I came home from work to find her sitting on the sofa with a tight expression on her face. The flat looked odd but I couldn't place why. She told me she was leaving, that she was in love with someone else and that was that. It was only after she'd closed the door behind her that I realised that all her stuff had already been packed up and removed. My ego was bruised, sure, but when she'd gone, there was nothing about her that I suddenly craved. I was free to have you and you were everything. I wish you could understand that. Still you doubt sometimes, which is ridiculous. How can you imagine that I'd want anyone else?

You hated my flat. Christ, the sulks and battles because of that place. Your silences and long baths that were just an excuse to punish me. I'd ask and ask what's wrong and you'd say, 'Nothing ignore me, I'm being stupid' and then finally you'd admit it was something you'd found – a hair clip left in the fruit bowl or junk mail arriving with her name on or photos that reminded you that my place had once been mine and Lucy's home. It pained you that she and I lived in that flat together, that we'd decorated the rooms one by one, that we'd chosen the furniture, cheap as it was, you saw meaning and significance in the smallest detail, in things that didn't matter in the least to me. It was all just things. You imagined a history for everything; the smallest object suddenly carried weight, as if a significant memory was attached to the most banal thing. You said you hated our muted and low-key taste – the beige walls and the pine coffee table. You hated the leather armchair we'd found in an antique shop in Rye. You hated the plain white totally inoffensive coffee mugs, saying they were bland beyond belief. You hated the plants that crowded the kitchen window ledge and the bonsai tree she'd bought me one Christmas.

You wanted to know which rooms we'd had sex in, if we'd fucked on the sofa, if we'd fucked on the kitchen counter, if we'd fucked in the shower. You wanted to raze it all to the ground. Lucy, Lucy, Lucy. Her memory tormented you, so I cleaned her out because I wanted to please you, because I loved you. I painted the walls the colours you chose, bright primary colours that seemed better suited to a children's nursery than our home, but I didn't care because you liked them and you were happier. I bought new furniture, replaced perfectly adequate things with different perfectly adequate things. I threw out photos of good times with family and friends because Lucy was in them. I did everything I could think of because I loved you and wanted to please you. Eventually I even sold the place at a loss so that we could move somewhere new and untainted. I excised an entire chunk of my life because it only mattered that you were in it

81

right now, I didn't need a history because I had a future with you and that future, stretching ahead of us, shiny and promising, was all I needed, all I wanted. So we bought the place in Clapham, together, both our names on the deed. You said you felt cleansed; that you could relax now that Lucy wasn't tainting everything. It was as if she was haunting you like a ghost. Except of course, she was alive and well, married to the guy she'd been screwing behind my back and the mother of four kids.

You have to see that I can't lose you now. After everything we've been through. Now we have a history as well as a future. Maybe we need counselling. Sally said it could work, that she and David saw someone after she had the kids and they'd run into problems. She said they've never been closer since then. She wonders if you've had post-natal depression since Jessica was born. It's possible. You could see a different doctor this time, maybe this time it will be better. They aren't infallible. I should take you again. How many times have I sat there, on those uncomfortable plastic chairs, flicking through old magazines and NHS pamphlets advising me on flu jabs, addiction and contraception? Watching the patients shuffling in and then out, clutching their prescriptions. Being a parent seems to be a continual back and forth to the doctors – for colds, chicken pox, innoculations, antenatal checks, post-natal checks and bumped heads. But that time you went in by yourself and I sat in the waiting room. You didn't want me to come in. I sat there reading the battered old magazines wondering what you needed privacy for, what you were telling him that I couldn't hear.

You were in there for ages; people came and went, looking at me sitting there alone. The receptionists answering the phones and booking appointments kept glancing over as if they'd forgotten why I was there and wondering if they should call security. When you came out you were grim-faced, furious, though I could see you'd been crying. You pulled your black raincoat tight around your body and threw your handbag over your shoulder. When I *asked what the doctor had said you muttered under your breath and then turned to me and said, 'Nothing, he didn't bother to listen, he didn't listen at all, he just made fucking assumptions. He gave me a prescription for these, bloody idiot.' You held the scrap of paper up so that I could see – Zoloft – and then tore it up and threw the pieces in the bin. You refused to discuss it except to say that you weren't depressed, that you didn't need pills and that the fucking doctor was wrong.*

But it's possible that you're depressed, isn't it? Maybe working and having the kids is too much for you. You aren't the expert, he is. Maybe all you need is a course of anti-depressants. Perhaps we need to go back to the doctor. There's no shame in it. Sally says it's very common now. Even she sometimes finds coping hard and she's a real trooper, as you know. She's a natural and even she finds it hard. You could give up your job, stay home with the kids; we can afford it. You'd love that, and so would the kids. A period of recuperation. A rest. No more full-time nursery for Jess. You could relax at home; Jess could go to nursery one day a week so you can go for lunch and shopping with your friends. I want you to be happy. This doesn't do anyone any good, all this silence and denial. I want to shake you, wake you up and force you to talk. I don't. I'm afraid of what you'll say. But honestly, it doesn't matter; it doesn't matter because I love you and we can work it through. If you could just tell me where I'm going wrong, I'd fix it. I'll change if it will make you happy.

It is hot, with few clouds cluttering the sky. The woman blinks in the hard light – the blink erases the world, only for it to reappear unchanged. A moment of blindness. She is sitting in a garden chair, reading a magazine. She is relaxing. She never leaves this domain. Her small world of anatomy, botany, butchery, economics. There is no other world than this. She is appearing in a dream.

Cora looks at her mother; she is a child, and the mother young again. Everything is recognisable: the old house, the metal-framed chair, the earthenware mug her mother always drank her tea from. She is watching, replaying an old scene. She has a puppy, a white fluffy terrier, small enough to carry around in her arms. He is called Bobby in the dream. She is sitting on her swing that hangs from the tree. Her feet scuff the ground beneath, obliterating the lawn. She is wearing her favourite shoes with brass buckles.

Bobby the puppy is lying on the path towards the house, his feet kicking, dreaming of rabbits. He is chasing them down dream holes, seizing them by their meaty back legs. Cora runs towards him as her mother turns another page. Blinking out the world. She wants him to wake up so she can play with him, dress him in doll's clothes and parade him as her little baby. The dream jumps frame. Bobby is on his side, rigid muzzle open at the hinge, his long tongue grey and slack. His feet continue to kick. Green foam pumps from his throat, collecting around the points of his teeth. Cora screams and her mother runs over to her and the dying dog.

'Mummy, fix him! Mummy, fix him, now!' she repeats, over and over. Her mother stands there, crying. They are both crying.

'I don't know what to do. I don't know what to do. Oh God, I don't know what to do.' Bobby is dead. Her mother blinks, the entire world caught in her eyelashes.

Cora sleeps on, her head heavy on the pillow.

I'm angry with you. I'm really fucking angry with you. Though I try so fucking hard not to be. I just want you to tell me what the fuck is going on. Who is he? I can't believe I'm putting up with all this. I've a lot to put up with too. I'm unhappy too. This silent treatment is killing me. Night after night I lie here and imagine these stupid fucking conversations with you. I'm doing my best to be patient and kind. I'm trying, I'm really trying to be the husband you need. But it's getting harder and harder. You treat me as if I'm a bastard, and you know you really are difficult sometimes. You are not perfect: you can be hard to love, hard to be around. I don't complain. I do my best by you and the children. I've never mentioned this before because I rarely admit it to myself because I feel disloyal and I don't want to hurt you, but there have been times when you've been an embarrassment, when you've humiliated me and our friends. If I'm really honest I know why we don't see people anymore, it's just too difficult to say openly, to your face.

Sometimes it's as if you don't like people. Even our good friends. You can be so rude. I say sometimes, but let's face it: you're rude when you have a drink. I don't even know you then. You're a fucking stranger to me. My God, Sandra's dinner party to celebrate her 36th birthday was ghastly. Jeremy and Gregor were there and Joanna showed up with her new man. Everyone was having a great time, drinking and eating and you were being your usual elegant, quietly funny self until the end, when Jeremy opened the last bottle of champagne. I looked at you and could see you were pissed. Your eyes rolled and your head tilted on your neck. You looked like a broken doll. A slice of chocolate cake sat uneaten on the plate in front of you. We all knew what you could be like, that you could be a little aggressive when drunk, but you were among friends and so I didn't think to take you home. I didn't want to embarrass you by treating you like a

85

naughty little girl I had to put to bed. Besides, until that point you'd been charming, there was no reason to imagine that you'd lash out. So I didn't imagine you'd tap on your glass and wait for quiet before you began telling us that after a lot of thought, your grand ecological solution would be to annihilate the population of Russia or China and sterilise 50% of the remaining humans left on earth. And I didn't imagine that when Sandra questioned you and asked if you were serious, you would answer 'Yes, and it's idiots like you that I'd sterilise first.'

Jesus, Cora. Everyone was quiet, shocked into silence. Sandra sat there completely taken aback, worse for wear herself and you started laughing. You just laughed in her face. Then you turned on Jeremy and Gregor calling them pretentious little queens and you told Joanna's boyfriend that she was a slut and he should be careful. You didn't say anything to me, but you stared at me across the table as if daring me to do something. You looked like a petulant child willing me to spank you so you could run and tell tales on me. Everyone else was looking at me too, wanting me to shut you up. As if you were my responsibility. What could I do? We all knew you were drunk and just trying to be shocking, but it was terrible, like you were finally expressing this dreadful rage that you'd kept pent up for years and years. I wondered if deep down you meant everything you'd said. That you hated us all and had nothing but contempt for us. You were filled with bitterness, but sober you could be the most gentle, loving woman. You aren't that person. I know you aren't. That isn't you.

The next morning you couldn't remember what you'd done. When I told you what you'd said you thought I was lying and started to cry. You sent flowers and cards to the others and they were good and forgave you because we're all old friends and that's what good friends do, but things had changed. We've seen less and less of our old gang. Now it's just you, me and the kids. Our world has shrunk. We don't talk about these things, or rather you won't talk about these things.

We all have our moments. I know I can be difficult. I can be grumpy sometimes. I want you to see that I do try though. That I forgive and keep on trying. I try to understand. It isn't easy. If you would only trust me enough to share your worries with me, maybe I could help. I would at least know what you were going through. The drinking worries me. Perhaps we should both stop. For the sake of the kids.

You know my grandfather was a drunk: he used to spoil Christmas every year until my father said enough was enough and banned my mother from inviting him. What I remember most about the old man is his smell, a stench of stale whisky, cigars and body odour. That and his hairy nostrils, which seemed to me to make perfect sense when I was a child: to be smelly but unable to smell oneself past the wads of hair stuffed up one's nose. Once the old man put his cigar out on the oven-ready turkey. My mother was in tears. She said her father hated her. Imagine that, thinking your parent hated you. Who hates their own children?

His father, my great-grandfather, was a convict. Probably never told you that. We never talk about any of this. I think the whole family is caught up in the shame, or maybe we just don't want to hurt my mother by bringing it all back up. Let sleeping dogs lie, that's what they say, isn't it? He was caught embezzling money from his company and sentenced to eight years. My mother thought that was the explanation for her father's drinking. Having a father in jail and a mother who could barely cope with life on her own. He lived with his granny, after his mother disappeared with a soldier. It does explain a lot: his father in prison, his mother running off, him left with his gran. He beat his wife. Mum saw it all. She once said her earliest memory was sitting in his car outside the pub with a glass of lemonade while he got pissed inside. Her mother was in the hospital. Mum would've been around seven years old, she said. He was a solicitor. Ironic huh? His dad a criminal, and he a lawyer. A drunkard who beat his wife and left his only daughter waiting for him while he got *drunk with his friends. I don't remember my granny much, not mum's mum anyway, she died when I was young, probably worn out with loving him, poor thing. There are photos though; Sally looks like her, tall and slender with the long, melancholy nose.*

You can understand why mum is the way she is though, right? It couldn't have been easy for her. She made sure our lives were very different. Sally and I had a very different family life. We grew up in such peace and stability in comparison to her. Mum and dad rarely argued; they were very loving with each other and us. It was perfect in a way, about as good as one can hope for. You see every family has their problems, their secrets. Perhaps knowing all these things means that we can make more allowances for one another. Perhaps knowing this will show you that you can trust me. I won't let you down. Nothing is perfect, but we have to try.

He is looking forward to the weekend. He said to Cora 'I can't wait for the weekend. I'm so tired, I don't know what's wrong with me.' Cora agrees because it's for the best that she does. But she hates Sundays and therefore the day preceding, with its gathering of dread. She hates the Day of Rest and its declaration of man's stupidity. What a stupid lack of confidence, to need a god to decree that humans need a day to rest. And with God involved one dare not disobey. You have no choice but to sit and eat and watch TV with your family, even now that God has fallen silent. Because to rest is to be with your family. It has been decreed. The only release is work, where you can be alone.

The train doors slide back with a hiss. She has dropped the children off at their schools. She is alone. A press of other solitary people moves her body into the train. She stands by the glass partition next to the seats, supported by the others travelling to work. The comforting warmth of their bodies lulls her; she wants to sleep in this upright embrace. The train moves and she is rocked back and forth. Closing her eyes she hears the muffled sounds of music being channelled into other ears, the muted rustle of paper and the strut of the wheels on the tracks. All the sounds must traverse the barrier of her solitude. She is suspended, separated from the world around her, not yet alive.

The doors open and more people push onto the train. She is held tighter, constricted by their bodies. Her proximity to them gives her a new privacy, she is known to them only as mass, as material, anonymous. Someone behind her breathes; she feels the expansion of their chest and the warm air on her neck. She can't move her arms without disturbing the passengers around her. Her body is useless, nothing but fat, muscle and bone. Tissue poised to rot; she is perfectly impotent and unthinking.

It is nine thirty. She has called work and told them she won't be coming in. She is at home, with a headache. Cora is missing. She exists in two places and is in neither. She hopes her husband doesn't call her at the office. It isn't likely; he will be too busy making the right impression in his job. He will think of her, though, and the children; he will mention them fondly to his colleagues should the opportunity arise. They are always with him. He has photos in his wallet to keep them safe. The train pulls into the station. The doors open after a pause, the passengers move forwards, impatient, ready to brisk towards their next connection. Cora lingers, not wanting the chill of standing upright without them. She wants them to stay, pressed together. Like hibernating mammals, curled around one another in a blood-warm den. Neutralised, heartbeats slowed, breathing in perfect time together.

The city clings to the earth. She walks out of the station into the street. She has no destination in mind, no plan, except to walk and walk. It is dry and warm. She carries a small black handbag, wears flat shoes and a grey dress that hangs in folds around her body. She wraps her arms around herself, holding herself in, restraining herself from running ahead, from getting lost. She moves forwards, in amongst all the bodies. The street is crowded, but less than it would have been only thirty minutes before. Others are in work. Making tea, typing, pushing information around, making visits to the stationery cupboard, to the toilet.

She waits to cross the street. Patience is key. Cars pass, taxis, a small crowd gathers behind her waiting for the machinery of the city to whirr into the next phase, to turn red, and hold back the traffic. The marvellous compliance of every one of them, maintaining order and safety, performing their role perfectly. The cars halt, the engines ticking. Cora crosses the street. She turns left, past a large church famous for its relics, its collection of miraculous body parts safe in gold caskets, then right into the next street. She passes a museum, also famous for its relics. She continues on. She doesn't rush, she doesn't linger. She walks. There are no children, unlike the suburbs where children proliferate. Children rule the outskirts of the city but are not welcome here in the centre.

She remembers the histories of the place from her schooldays, the legends of fires and plagues, bombs and beheadings. Whole ranks of horses slaughtered. Babies dropped in gutters, old women buried alive. Lies, all lies. There isn't a single speck of dust on Cora; she is untouched by the elements. She is entirely clean here in the perfect peace of the city. Completely anonymous, she is reduced to a female body that walks, that carries a bag, that wears shoes, that wears clothes. That is how she is defined, at that moment. She is nothing else. She turns her wrist towards her, checking her watch: she has six hours. Six hours of peace. Six hours of being no one at all. If she is noticed by anyone else, it won't matter, because they will have no idea of what she is. Except the bag, the dress, the shoes, her flesh. A collection of materials amongst other materials: concrete, glass, and stonework, wood, plastic. Solid.

Her steps are precise. She is well-practised. She is hungry, or rather, her body is hungry. Her stomach coils and flexes. She decides to ignore it. She does not want to be noticed by anyone. She does not want to enter a café or restaurant and speak to a single other human. She passes shops with large plate glass windows, filled with treasures and people. She is immune. There is nothing she wants, just to walk alone. A fear flashes through her mind – what if she walks out of the city, if she runs out of space? She'll turn and walk back, she reasons, but then she might be noticed. She forgets that she will run out of time before she runs out of space. Silly fear. Silly thought. She reports back to herself. I won't run out of streets...I will run out of time!

She moves forward. This street is more crowded: she is jostled occasionally, a shoulder catches hers, knocks her back a little. Other bodies recognise her shape, but they do not see her. She pushes on, felt but not seen, not looked at. Ushered on by the crowd and the traffic lights, the flow of movement, she floats along. She is a mark on the city. A blot. She is not bothered by the shoves and bumps from elbows, shoulders and carrier bags. She is grateful. Her arms hang by her side. She is unarmed, unguarded. She is a leaf floating on the surface, carried along in the currents, weightless and inconsequential. Doors open from the shops and the cafes into the street. Bodies join the crowd, bodies leave; cold air pumps out along with music. The doors shut. She is nearly at the end of the road. Ahead is the park. She moves towards it.

The grass has withered in the heat. The soil is compacted dust, easily kicked up. She walks towards a tree. It reaches out overhead, its large branches braced. It is a picture book tree, an absolute tree. She sits under it and leans her back against the trunk. She is uncomfortable: the large roots protrude from the ground and press into her buttocks. She stays where she is. It isn't necessary to be comfortable. Picking up a fallen twig she picks at the end. It isn't solid: the wood is made up of fibres, like threads twisted together, a matrix. She picks the twig apart, peeling back the filaments. She can't imagine solidity, what a comfort that would be, a solid mass instead of granulation and particles. Something rigid and defined, not reliant on anything else at all – completely differentiated from the world around it. Indestructible. Leaning back now on the tree she feels its fragility, a composite of parts, unrecognisable. Even a tree disappoints.

A woman walks past with a child in a pushchair. The child looks too large to still be in a buggy. They cross to a bench opposite Cora. The woman sits down and turns the buggy away from her. Reaching into a large bag she pulls out an orange. The dark-haired woman begins to peel the orange, taking care to remove the coarse white pith. All the while she is chatting to the child; Cora can hear her voice undulating across the still grass. She is singing a nursery rhyme. The child kicks its feet in time with the song. The woman hands the child a segment of the orange. It raises its small fist to its mouth. They are not aware that Cora watches them. She is still picking at the shards of wood in her hand. She works at her nail. Unthinking, repetitive and soothing gestures. Prising the hard shell from its bed. Small miracles of pain.

The woman on the bench reaches to the child and undoes the strappings of the pushchair. The child is freed, and placed on its feet toddles around, bending from the waist as if hinged, picking up dirt and filth from the floor. The woman follows it, still talking to the child, guarding the toddler from harm. Coming closer, the child walks in the direction of Cora and the tree; it bends to pick a daisy, its head too big for its fat little body. Cora can see the child clearly now. It is a monster, a genetic mishap. Its large tongue protrudes from its mouth. Its disfigurements privilege it amongst other children. It is a marvel, a brilliant mistake, a one in a million. Cora feels a dull jolt of jealousy for the mother. For her damaged progeny.

Cora could love her children if they were deformed. She has always been moved by images of starving or disabled children. Her children, with their strutting perfection, reject her, they don't need her attentions, they aren't endangered by the weight of oxygen or the movement of sleep. She could adore a damaged little baby, beholden only to mother love. A baby with the bones of a bird or an eggshell skull. A double-headed monster baby, fused in the womb with its dead twin. How much easier it would be to love the chaos of damaged limbs than the gurgling perfection of a normal baby. An ordinary baby wrapped in woollen clothing.

The splinter of wood is sharp under her nail. She rolls it back and forth, loosening the flesh from the nail, excavating the raw pink underneath. The succulent clam tight in its shell. She breathes, new filtered air rushes in. The mother tucks her contorted child away into its carriage. They saunter away, singing a new nursery rhyme. Blood bubbles up from the wooden spear Cora has dug into her finger. More people are gathering in the park. Lunchtime. Groups congregate around plastic bags filled with packets of sandwiches and cans of drink, they laugh and joke together. The summer is a carnival, life restates itself, and they kid themselves they belong somewhere. One or two lone picnickers lay back with their eyes closed, or read a book. Music plays from a portable stereo. A single airplane coasts overhead, its engine sound muffled by distance. Closing her eyes, Cora tears the nail off her finger.

Her hand takes shape in her mind. Her nerve endings contact her brain, information is exchanged. She stands, dropping the nail on the grass and wrapping her finger in a tissue from her handbag. Blood oozes through and she is careful not to touch her dress. It would be no good stained. The nail lies on the grass, a monument to her presence. Her DNA scattered like seed on the soil. She imagines it taking root and producing small yellow fruits, bitter-tasting, with withered flesh. She walks, this time in another direction. Stepping carefully over the reclining diners. Her bag over her shoulder. She walks towards the meld of modern and old buildings, thrilling to the agony collected in her fingertip. She is unified by the pain: whole, newly named – baptized. She forgets what she was. What she failed to be. This is happiness. She has managed to arrive via a circuitous route. She is full to the brim. Cora overflows with pain and joy.

Now, she knows exactly where she is going. She walks quickly, before time runs out. She knows these streets well. She worked here when she first left university. She turns left and avoids stepping into dog shit. She rushes towards pain, so as to inflict it on herself first before any other cunt gets the chance. As she moves she taps at her wounded finger with her thumb, pressing it with her nail, releasing little pumps of clarity. She breathes. Turns into the small street market, walking past the stalls piled with sooty fruit and vegetables. Her finger has swollen slightly, and responds to her prodding with new blood. It soaks the tissue wrapped around it. A thickset man steps towards her smiling, looking her up and down. He likes what he sees and wants her to buy some flowers from him. He proffers a bunch of cheap chrysanthemums wrapped in cellophane. The flowers send messages from behind their protective window. He wants her to buy his flowers and let him stroke her breasts; he'd like to feel her body underneath her dress. She knows what men think. She can see his thoughts projected onto his face. The flowers tell her. She looks through him at the road ahead. He turns away, looking for his next punter. She can see clearly.

A cluster of mini-theatres crowds the end of the street. In the doorway of each one a woman stands, a thick layer of make-up competing with her skin. They all wear miniskirts and bra-tops, and look bored and at ease with their semi-nudity. They beckon to passers-by, inviting them in to watch the live sex or striptease shows. Cora would like to go in, but doesn't dare. She would like to be a man and to have all the mysteries of other female bodies solved. She would like to see the wads of cellulite and fat on other thighs, watch the judder of breasts as the male crashes his body against the female. To sit at the front and smell them, hear them. To be so close as to see the hard skin on the balls of their feet, the thin skin on the backs of their knees. The exits and entrances. She would like the world to reveal itself to her. But she is too afraid to look. She can only watch it on films. Removed from her own body, mediated by the protective intervention of a lens.

She enters a shop with blacked-out windows. A young woman with purple hair, dressed in a black leather mini-dress, is standing behind a counter reading a book. Behind her is a display cabinet with dildos of various shapes, sizes and colours. Shelves of films line the black walls and, in the centre of the shop, racks are hung with clothes made from leather, nylon and rubber. A hand-written sign saying 'Toys and Equipment' points to a flight of stairs. There are a couple of other customers, men, browsing through the films. They stand carefully reading the description on the back of each case. Cora moves quickly. Her cheeks flare red. Looking up, she realises she hasn't been noticed. She is another customer, no more and no less. No one remarks on her presence. They are perhaps too polite, or too busy with their own shopping trip to care.

The floor is carpeted; she is surprised by how clean it is. Her breath slows, she moves towards the clothes, looking through the outfits, one by one. Her injured finger catches in the lacework of a nipple-less bra. She sucks in sharp pleasure and is reassured. She is a thing that responds. She is in a world mysterious to her. She looks around, but can't see straight. She is less sure now of what she wants, but knows she will find it here. The shop is not what she's always imagined. Far calmer and more professional than she thought, it smells of a pine air freshener, or disinfectant. She is impressed by its hygiene. A radio tuned to a pop station chatters over by the cash desk. She picks up a shiny white plastic nurse's outfit complete with hat and stethoscope. She wonders if her husband would like her to wear it. She wonders if she would like to wear it, how it would feel on her skin. Whether they would indulge in role-play. He asked her to, once: he wanted her to dress up as a secretary and sit on his knee. He offered to dress up for her too, in exchange, but she couldn't think of anything she would like. He was enough then, his flesh, his smell, his weight. But she dressed up, in a pencil skirt and prim blouse, wearing stockings for him and black silk underwear. She sat on his knee, feeling ridiculous as he called her 'Miss Jones' and asked her to take dictation. She wasn't enough; that was the message. Only make-believe can satisfy. She put the nurse's outfit back on the rack.

'Can I help you find something?' The shop assistant walks over, her legs bare except for the leather boots. She speaks with a soft lilting accent, difficult to place but instantly soothing. Cora looks at her, at her full lips and round chin. She is pretty beneath her uniform of cosmetics and trashy clothes, her limbs smooth-skinned and long. She's taller than Cora in her high-heeled boots, as tall as a man. She places her hand on the rail of clothes, the nails dirty and short like a little girl's. Cora wants the hand to stroke her own hand; she wants to be held by the girl, placated and kissed. She has the feeling the girl could help her, but she doesn't know what kind of help she needs or even how to begin to ask. This other body standing so close to her is a body for which Cora is not a means of fulfilment or nourishment: they are completely separate. She is a customer, she has a role negotiated and understood, fully legislated.

'I'm not sure what I'm looking for, I'm sorry, I'm just browsing.'

The girl moves a little closer to Cora. One of the other customers leaves the shop, the bell above the door noting his departure. The door closes, sealing them in again.

'Well, are you looking for a costume, or lingerie?'

'No, no I don't think so.'

'What about a vibrator? We've got some great ones in stock.'

'I think I'd like something for my nipples.' The words squirm on Cora's tongue.

'To use alone or with a partner? We have booby drops in chocolate, strawberry and passion fruit flavours. We have nipple clamps, nipple weights, vibrating nipple clamps, suction pumps.'

'I'm not sure. Clamps I think. Or something like that.'

The shop assistant steps back, smiling, revealing a row of perfect teeth.

'Come with me, I'll show you what we've got.' She walks back to the counter and bends down, leaning into the space beneath the counter top and cash till. Standing, she begins laying out objects. The clamps catch the light, shiny metal contraptions that look like medical equipment. Cora watches as the girl displays them like fine jewellery.

'OK. So we have these ones, they're good for beginners; they're adjustable here and have these little rubber bits so they won't be too harsh. Then moving up in intensity we have these ones with little spikes, again these can be adjusted so you can get used to the sensation gradually; you can also add weights to these. We have these that are, I think very prettily, joined with a chain that dangles down on your chest and can be pulled to add to the sensation. Then these ones that squash the nipple between these two plates that are moved by turning this screw. And then we have these ones that are super intense.' She held up a pair of silver metal vices. 'You tighten the two plates around the nipple, with this little ball on the side and the points of these spikes cut into the skin. So these ones crush and bite into the nipple, a double sensation I suppose. These ones aren't for amateurs really.'

Cora looks at the clamps in front of her, the world outside the shop evaporating. The other customer moves in behind her. She can smell his cologne.

'Can I pay for these please?' He hands over two DVD's. On the cover of one Cora can see photos of beautiful young men posing with each other, their perfect bodies flexed and bulging. Cora moves to one side, stepping out of the customer's way. The films disappear into a black plastic carrier bag.

'£25 please.' The girl rings them into the old fashioned till. He hands her cash, untraceable to an account. Leaving no paper trail. His gold wedding ring cutting into his finger. She hands over the merchandise and he thanks her. As he turns to go he nods at Cora.

'So, what do you think? Any of these look good? I've got vibrating ones too.' The sales pitch is seamless; the girl's knowledge of her stock impresses Cora, because Cora knows little about anything, least of all herself. The girl looks at her, her black-rimmed eyes scanning her face. She's not unfriendly, curiosity guides her. 'Shall I let you think for a minute?' She turns and picking up a can of furniture polish and a rag begins cleaning the shelves behind her. Picking up each dildo and dusting under it, before flicking the duster over the rubber rod itself. Cora extends the fingers on her unharmed hand. She touches the silver implements; they're cool and clinical. She runs her nail along the jagged edge of one of the clamps, its jaws crammed with teeth.

In Argentina, Orcas beach themselves to catch seal pups. She saw them on TV. They launch themselves on the shale, against their instincts, their bulk slapping into the shore, thrusting the water ahead of them. They grab the baby in their jaws, the sharp points of their teeth puncturing blubber, before turning and turning, working their mass forwards and back, turning at last with the tidal inrush and swimming back out to their family group with the drowning pup. Helped by the geological construction of the beach, they roll back out to sea on the perfectly round pebbles, transferred back from the alien land as if on ball bearings. It isn't all in their favour: it's dangerous and sometimes they miss, hauling themselves back off the beach without a catch. To the scientists that watch them, they are miraculous. Though scientific scrutiny doesn't allow for miracles, privately the scientists worship the animals and their intelligence. Giving each one a name and creating a history for them. They breach rational protocols. The scientists kid themselves that they have translated the whistles and squeaks of the whales' language. Cora understands this need to know something absolutely and imagines that the knowing would be miraculous.

The girl turns back, a leather-clad housewife, clutching her cleaning apparatus.

'Well, what do you think?'

Cora's injured finger throbs, it soothes her. She recognises the boundary of her self.

'I want something discreet, that I can wear under clothes and not be noticed.' She is surprised by her own voice, surprised by knowing exactly what it is she came for all along.

'OK, what about this?' The girl reaches back under the counter and pulls out a small black box. Lifting the lid she reveals two small clamps, similar to the others already on the counter. There isn't much variety in human joy. 'These ones are adjustable by turning this screw just like the others, but they lie flat against the skin so if you wore a bra over them they wouldn't be seen. I guess you shouldn't wear them for too long though, I mean they could cut off the blood supply.'

'I'll take them. How much are they?'

'These ones are £40. Are you interested in any other bondage or S and M toys?'

'Pardon?' Cora breathes in her new complicity with the girl, the place, this world.

'S and M. We've got lots of great dungeon equipment. We've got a few doms on our client list, so we have some great pieces. They're like art. Really beautiful.'

'No, not today, another time.' Cora takes her purse from her bag, exposing her injured hand to the sales girl.

'That looks nasty. What happened there?'

'Nothing, just a silly accident.' Cora handed the girl the cash. They can't afford this. Him and her, their joint finances could only stretch so far. She shouldn't be spending money on something so disgusting, so selfish. The rot has set in. She must try to hold it back, or cut it out like a tumour; she must work to stop the decay. She should find other ways to answer herself. But it's done. The money has gone. The girl hands her a black carrier bag. She could change her mind. But how embarrassing, the girl would be annoyed. She's rung it through the till now. And so too late. She can't go backwards. This is what she has chosen. She turns and walks out the door. The street is exactly as she left it.

Her time is up. She hurries towards the station, the black bag shrinking her attentions. It swings gaily by her side. To and fro. It skips and twitches with her footsteps as if it were alive. She hurries, knowing relief is captured in the box. She has found a way to manage. To call herself back from the dead at a twist of the screw. She looks where she is going, recognising everything she sees, knowing the names of objects, of places. Life, her life anyway, unlike books or films, doesn't have a particularly significant moment, a revelation, a turning, when things started to waver, there was no definitive moment when the change occurred. Not even this event. She is an accumulation of small moments. One breath after another, shuffling in and out through her nose. All she can think of is forgetting. Of returning.

The station is jammed with commuters. She can't avoid them; she must get on the train at the right time. She checks her phone. No calls. Not from him, nor her work. She has made it. She is exhausted, her feet and back throb deliciously. Her body is entirely hers. The message board indicates her train is in and ready for boarding. She pushes forwards, in a rush for home. Now she has the means to transform her guilt and shame she can go back. She flashes her pass at the barrier, automatic arms swing open, she is admitted, she belongs, she has her ticket; there will be no keeping her out now. She toes the line.

It was raining on our wedding day. It was also raining when I proposed to you and you said no. I'd taken you to Paris. Is that a cliché, to go to Paris? Probably, I never was very good at these things. Anyway, we were in Paris, we wandered around the galleries and walked halfway up the Eiffel Tower before you got too scared. We took a boat trip down the Seine and got drunk over lunch in a café. Then, finally, I took you to dinner and, after eight courses of food that baffled us both, I got down on one knee, proffering the carefully chosen ring. You said no. Do you remember? I wonder if you do remember. It often seems that the details of our life together are beyond you – forgotten and meaningless. Even the most important and supposedly significant are beneath your radar now. You forgot our anniversary. You said you didn't, said that you'd left my card at work but I could tell by the look on your face that you'd forgotten when I gave you your card and flowers. It feels as if you're fumbling your way through our marriage. Hands outstretched, your eyes closed.

When we first met you told me how superstitious you were. How you saluted magpies and threw spilled salt over your shoulder. How you never walked under ladders, or put shoes on a table or let knives cross at the blade or left a hat on the bed. You said a bird trapped in the house was a dire portent that warned of the death of someone close. You read the world as if it were sending you signals. It made me laugh, it seemed so at odds with you, with who I thought you were, clever and logical and stridently atheist, but still it was charming, and you could've done anything and I'd only have loved you more.

So, you couldn't say yes to my proposal on a rainy day you said, you said it didn't bode well for our future. You made me wait for sunshine, and do the whole thing again. So I finally proposed a few days later, back at home in less glamorous Clapham, when the sun was finally shining and you'd got up and had a shower and I'd made you tea and toast and I asked you again, kneeling on the chilly kitchen floor, and this time you said yes. The ring was too big for your tiny finger, but you didn't mind. We went back to bed and celebrated over and over. Your lovely arms around me. Kissing your neck, your hair still damp, your legs wrapped around me, holding you, my hands on your bottom pulling you closer, your feet digging in, pulling me in tighter, as if we couldn't possibly be close enough.

I got dressed and ran to the corner shop to buy the only bottle of champagne they had. You called your parents and then I called mine. We threw a party at our new flat and everyone came and you wore that black velvet dress with a slit all the way up to your thigh. You didn't drink too much. Your dad gave a toast and pressed an envelope with cash into our hands. He held you close to him, his arm around your waist, while I said thanks and everyone cheered and your mother stood quietly next to you both, round like a ball in a blue and cream dress with her tight curls like a helmet on her head. She'd made us a cake, heart-shaped and pink with our names iced on in white. My mother thought it was twee and laughed about it all night. We cut it together, my hand gripping yours, you gripping the knife, in a rehearsal of our wedding day, while everyone took photos and cheered.

It rained on our wedding day, and I was afraid you'd say no at the altar. We'd even joked about it, how all that planning and expense would be in vain just because of the weather. You didn't of course, not even you were that superstitious. In your white dress and blue shoes. Your hair all piled up on your head and threaded with flowers. You whispered 'Do I look stupid?' as we stood together at the altar and I shook my head. If I'm honest, I think all brides look a little silly and nothing at all like themselves, but who would say it? Especially after all that money and planning and time. And anyway, you were marrying me and that was all I cared about. We could've got married just the two of us alone wearing jeans and I'd have been happy.

As it was it was still pretty small, much to my mother's disapproval. I think she was hoping for a huge formal bash that she could invite her friends to, with a toastmaster and four courses for dinner. She even offered to hire a marquee and have the reception in their garden. You said no. You were adamant that we'd have a small, intimate wedding in the hotel near your parents' house. I'm not sure if that was to save your father's pride or because that's genuinely what you wanted. You said you weren't interested in placeholders and matching table linen and flower arrangements and all the other things that were deemed essential to successful nuptials. I didn't care how we did it, as long as we did it. It didn't matter to me that the food was ordinary or that the hotel's carpets were ancient and smelly or that the champagne ran out an hour earlier than predicted. You were my wife and I loved to say it. I would bring you up in conversations – my wife this, my wife that – because I was so proud.

People warn you that it can all go wrong, that marriages don't last anymore, that divorce is on the rise. But you don't think it will happen to you. Of course you don't. You think you will be the exception to prove the rule. I still think that. I don't care who he is, or even if there is someone else. We will get through this. We have to – it isn't about the two of us anymore, we're a family, a unit. And we must stay together.

I often think of our honeymoon. Fourteen days of immaculate pleasure. You even gave up smoking for me. For our future babies. We went to my parents' place in Mallorca and sunbathed naked by the pool. We fucked in the sea, your legs around my waist, your swimsuit pulled to one side. We got drunk on cocktails in the restaurants by the old port and chose lobsters from a tank for our dinner, which you then refused to eat in a fit of tearful guilt. We hired mopeds and scooted about the island till I crashed and skinned my elbow and knees and you deemed it too dangerous. We seem to have always had an incredible time together by the sea. Perhaps that's the answer, move to the seaside. Perhaps a change of scene would be good, a new start together.

Cornwall or Devon. We could buy a cottage, change careers, finally get a dog. We'd have room then and they're not as dirty or dangerous as you think. The kids would love it. We could find Patch a football club and Jess a ballet school; they'd make new friends quickly. All that space, the sea, more freedom, clean and safe. Away from the city and all its poisons. We could have chickens, grow our own fruit and veg; I could build the kids a tree house and a sand pit with a paddling pool. We could even have goats. I could work for myself, start a consultancy or an agency or something and you could stay at home with the kids and paint or take a course in art history. We could forget the past and begin again. We could have another baby. I think we could be happy away from here. Make a clean break together. Just us four and the new dog.

The house behind the door is silent. No one is home, she couldn't have wished for better. The black bag dangles from her wrist. Raps against her leg. She inserts her key and walks into the hallway. She scrapes her feet on the mat, rubbing off the dirt from the street. She doesn't want to walk it into the house. She wonders where they can all be, it's his turn to collect them. The car is on the drive; maybe they are at the park. He is good like that: he takes them out to play. He runs with them and falls over, throwing them into the air. Pushing them high on the swings. He is good. She has watched them, chasing round and round. He helps them climb to the top of the frame, calling encouragement and climbing up to rescue them when they get stuck and cry. Another sort of mother would tell him to be careful, would watch with her heart in her mouth. Another sort of woman would tell him to stop, let them catch their breath before tickling them almost to death. She doesn't, she says nothing. What she feels is the flattening of time. Her skin thickens like hide and she recedes, pulls back to where she can't hurt them. Too late though, the dirty deed's been done.

She walks through the hall to the kitchen. She will wait a moment before going upstairs and opening the little box inside the black plastic bag. She will wait just a moment. She will linger. She reaches to open the door with her intact hand. She hears a shuffle, some movement behind the door to the kitchen. The moment of expectation is puffed like dust into the air. She isn't alone. She has a premonition of what will happen next. She remembers what day it is. She composes herself, realigning her mechanism. She walks back to the bottom of the stairs and hangs up her handbag and the black plastic bag. Her liar's face settles. She walks back down the hall and opens the door. Surprise. Surprise.

The children leap from behind the curtains. Balloons in primary colours are Sellotaped to the wall and the back of the kitchen chairs. A shop-bought cake is perched on a silver board in the centre of the table. He steps forward to light the candles. Everyone is smiling. Cora is smiling. The two children, whose names are Patrick and Jessica, Patch and Jess – there, fixed into position by a name – run to her.

'We surprised you, Mummy! We surprised you!'

He walks to her, arms open, and pulls her to him. 'Happy Birthday, darling. I know you didn't want a fuss but we thought we'd surprise you.' He kisses the top of her head. His fingers rub her back, strumming against the strap of her bra as if she were an instrument. The divide isn't breached by his proximity. She stands, doing the right thing, conforming to what must be done.

'Blow out the candles, Mummy.' The children issue shrill demands, they're in charge here.

She obeys, leaning forward, her mouth puckered; she takes a deep breath and blows. She closes her eyes to make a wish. What could she wish for when she has everything anyone would want? Which anyone? Who? Whoever. She has what they want.

'What did you wish for? Did you wish for presents?'

Cora nods and, producing a smile, she reaches for the knife to cut the cake. Forgetting herself, she reaches with the wrong hand.

'Mum, what have you done to your finger?' They, the three of them, move in on her to see better.

'Darling, what happened?'

She reaches for the lie she prepared. 'I caught my finger in a door at work. It's OK, nothing to worry about. Honestly, it doesn't even really hurt anymore.'

'It looks very sore, Mummy. Did you cry?' The little girl is concerned, she looks at the wound like a mother, ready to comfort and mend.

Cora shakes her head. She wants to silence them and their inane questions. She wants them away from her. She slices into the cake, splitting the white sugar coating, dividing the words iced in pink across the surface, cutting letter from letter, until they're meaningless.

'Who wants a piece?'

The children yell 'me, me,' and she hands them the chunks of flour, fat and sugar. The husband tuts: cake before dinner and not even on plates. But it is a special treat. He lets it go. She spoils them. You spoil them. I spoil them.

'Let me have a look and put a plaster on for you.' He moves closer, reaching for her hand.

'No, I'll sort it later. It's fine, honestly.'

He is watching her, his expression entirely legible. His shoulders drop, his eyes droop, he sags under the weight of his theatrical sadness. He is sincere. Completely sincere.

'Why do you push me away, Cora? Let me help you.'

'Honestly, I'm fine. Let's enjoy my party, shall we?'

His hands drop to his sides. He will feel her rejection all evening but put on a show of bravery for the children. She sits down, tired. The party is over. She is coming apart, dismembered. The black bag and its contents are all she can think about. The children climb onto her lap. They love her, he loves her. Their love devours her; it roams about the house like a beast, ripping chunks from her body. She is the meat their love requires. The little girl pats Cora's face; her breath, sugar-rotten, makes Cora gag. The child has a clot of dried mucus in the corner of her eye. Cora wants to shove Jessica and her dirty fingers off her lap but she daren't move. The boy leans his head on her shoulders, lolling against her chest. Together their weight crushes her.

Behind the loving trio, he cooks the dinner. It's her favourite dinner. He knows this because he makes it for her over and over again and she always eats it. She might even lick the plate clean, though she never has before. There is a confusion of voices here. The chatter invades every pore. She will never be alone. There is no alone. He pulls the lasagne from the oven, placing it on the table with a flourish. She longs for the black bag. There is a salad, mixed and dressed with oil and vinegar, just as she likes it, and some garlic bread. A birthday feast. There will be no pudding, as he had intended that to be the cake, and she spoilt that plan. Never mind.

The children climb off her and into their designated seats, one each side of the table. Accordingly the parents sit at either end, as they should. She stands and moves to lay the table. He directs her to sit. This is her treat. She is to do nothing. Not a single thing. She is not to lift a finger, especially her wounded finger. She is to relax, bone idle for the rest of the evening. This will give her time to indulge herself in the luxury of her offspring. He pours her a glass of wine. She digs a serving spoon – a wedding gift from his parents – into the lasagne and drops some onto the little boy's plate.

'That's too much, Mummy.' She ignores him, and serves the girl. The children will not eat salad; they refuse what is good for them and gorge on disease-inducing rubbish. She serves herself a small portion before handing him the spoon.

'I should light some candles.' He jumps from his seat and rummages under the sink for candles and the candlesticks. An effort must be made to mark the occasion. He lights them and places them on the table, illuminating his handiwork. Shadows puppet their gestures on the wall. They eat. That is all they seem to do. I spend my life feeding them and when they've finished I feed them all over again. She feels sick. She wants to go upstairs and lie down. She wants to go upstairs and open the box that is in the black bag. She wants to not be the monster that she is. She finishes her wine. He pours her another. He doesn't spill a drop. He helps himself to more of the food. The children chatter, finish their supper and jump down from their seats. He clears the table; she must remain seated and enjoy her rest. It is her special day.

'Presents!' The children run in clutching brightly wrapped packages. 'We've got another surprise, Mummy!' They collide with her knees. He watches laughing, proud of them. Proud of this little scene. They tumble the presents into her lap. 'Open them! Open them now.' The boy thinks of nothing but acquisition, he is so desperate for her to tear the paper he'll do it himself if she doesn't get a move on. He steps from foot to foot, as if he wants to pee. She picks one up, squeezes it, shakes it; performs the expected pantomime of guessing what's inside the coloured paper. It flops like a dead fish in her hand. She lifts a corner of the paper and tears it back.

'What can this be?' She knows what it is. A scarf, a silk scarf. The type his sister wears. Something Cora has never worn. It's beautiful. She wraps it around her neck. 'Do I look pretty?'

'Yes, Mummy. You're very pretty.' Patrick leans in to kiss her. She turns her cheek. His damp kiss lands on her chin, leaving a sticky residue.

'Open the next one.' Jessica can't be left out. She must be acknowledged. Cora repeats the schtick again. Shaking and prodding the gaudy package. It's a box of chocolates.

'Chocolates! Are you going to share, Mummy? It's very naughty not to share.' Cora opens the lid of the box. They pounce, him and the children. They take a chocolate each. She is allowed the rest. They acquiesce that she ought to have all the others now, as they are her special treat.

'Do you like your party?' they ask.

Cora nods. The food is rising up her oesophagus, her stomach turning inside out.

'Shall we play a game? Because it is your party and Daddy said we could play a game after dinner.'

'OK, Patch. But choose one we can all play.' She says her lines with conviction. She is very convincing.

'Let's play Ludo. I'll go and get it.' Patrick runs with his sister trailing him upstairs to his room.

The husband comes to her and lays his hands on her shoulders. 'You OK, Cora? D'you like your presents? I wasn't sure what to get you.'

'Wonderful, thank you. I've had a nice time. Really, it's very thoughtful.' She is a hybrid of what she says and what she thinks. She is a half-breed.

The children come back; it's hard to keep up with their entrances and exits. But they come back clutching the game. It is seven o'clock. Nearly the children's bedtime. She can't wait. The game is unpacked. A jumble of counters and dice. She must pick a colour. Green. Green isn't a girls' colour. But she is allowed to have green, as it is her birthday. The game plays. The dice lands giving a six, then a four, then other numbers. Counters move forwards. Incremental. Time crawls on its belly.

'Mummy, your turn. Mummy!'

'Sorry, sorry. I was just thinking.'

'Mummy, play the game.' The little boy supervises the ordeal.

'Yes.' She throws a three and moves forwards. She is neither winning nor losing. Patrick takes his turn and then her husband. Jessica is losing the game. Her red counters lag behind. She cries. Her mouth wide open, her worn milk teeth on show, she ups the volume a notch. The sound campaigns against the barricade of the world outside her self. Her father finally reaches for her.

'Poor tired little bunny. It doesn't matter about the silly game. Come on now, dry your eyes.'

Cora doesn't move, doesn't want to see the child. She looks down at her finger. Clear fluid seeps from the wound and glistens in the candlelight. Healing fluid. She waits while he comforts the girl. Jessica calms down and hiccups her unfinished sobs. He is winning the game, with Patch a close second. Soon it will all be over. The game will be finished and she will be free for a moment or two. He wins. Both the children sulk, the burden of losing contorting their faces. Of course, he wouldn't let them win because that would teach them false values, and there is nothing more dangerous than that. Better to have a painful lesson from failure than to learn how to cheat.

He gives them a cup of milk each and refills her glass of wine. She feels drunk. She hasn't performed as she should have.

They are all disappointed, but they smile anyway because it's her birthday and they must be happy. She knows he watches her, missing nothing. Love provides an extra vigilance. One can't take anything for granted. She is depressed, that's obvious. Perhaps she is overworked, stressed. Maybe he should suggest she gave up her job. Allow her more time with the kids. He could work more hours. They could manage on his salary. Who knows what he thinks. She has no idea what he's really thinking.

He scoops up both children. 'Time for bed.' They reach for her. For kisses and cuddles. For what should come naturally. A love that excludes all violence, unshadowed by an opposite; it must be untainted by hate or even simple ambivalence. Therefore what's demanded is unnatural. Love is violence, wreaking havoc on her health with the dark sacrifice it demands.

He carries them both towards the door. He is strong enough; his arms encircle their bodies. Bodies that romp through her, to which she can have no resistance. Their little fingers rest on his neck; they are completely at ease, their bodies melding with each other. They are a fusion of molecules. They enjoy one another; even going to bed is fun when they are with him. He whispers something and they both giggle. They leave the room. He walks past the bag hanging on the banister. He doesn't notice it. Why would he? Why would he even for one minute imagine what sort of a woman he married? When she didn't even know herself.

Alone, she is aware only of her hatred. She hates them for being. They are hated for nothing at all. The sounds of their love for each other filter through the wood and plaster construction of the brittle house. They brush their teeth, they piss on the toilet, they make a mess. They get into bed, they sleep. Each one utterly mysterious. Every night the same routine. She listens to them; an ancient urge spreads itself through her body. As clean and pure as all instincts, bone deep. Her finger is clean and shiny, unprotected. The urge to destroy, thick as mucus, clogs her veins. With her fist she grabs a handful of her hair and rips it from her head. She clears the blockage. The urge fades. She hears lights snapping off. His tread on the stairs, descending from the children to her. She crosses the kitchen and drops the bundle of hair into the bin. She sits back down, the patch of scalp raw.

'Right, that's them off to sleep. Happy birthday, my love. What would you like to do now? Watch a film? Or listen to some music?' He sits in the chair opposite her, his hands folded on the table; he leans forward, towards her.

'I'm going to go up for a shower. OK? Thank you for the party. It was really sweet of you.' She stands up and turns for the door.

'Cora, don't go up just yet. Let's spend some time together. Seems like we're never alone anymore.'

'I'm tired, really. I'm sorry, another time, OK?' He reaches for her and closes his hand around her wrist. She wishes he'd squeeze it, yank her down, kick her, smash her head against the floor, punch her in the face. Punish her. He won't. He never would. He wouldn't hurt a fly, much less a woman, much less his wife. No matter what she said right now, no matter what she did, he wouldn't give her what she wants. She pulls away and he drops her arm.

'Cora, we need to talk. Let's talk. I want to talk. Please.' He stands and puts his hands on her shoulders. He does the right things, he looks into her face. He is sincere. His sincerity tickles her. She wants to vomit laughter, black violent spew. He is too good.

'Please. I'm tired, I've had a long day.' She looks up at him, making the effort to meet his eyes, to reassure him, waits for him to look away, or say something to break the moment she created.

'Is it me? Have I done something?'

'God, no. Of course you haven't. I'm just tired, please.'

'Cora. Something is wrong. You don't talk to me, you don't touch me. It's like you can't wait to get away from here. I can't

113

help but wonder.' His hands drop to his sides. He plays his part beautifully.

'Wonder what? What do you wonder?'

He breathes heavily, looks at his feet. 'Cora, is there someone else?'

'What? Oh Jesus Christ. No. No. Why would you say that? Christ, I'm just tired. Can't that be enough? Where would I find the time, or even the energy to have an affair?'

He sits in the chair, his body doubled over, leaning on his knees. Clasping his hands together.

'I'm sorry. I just can't imagine what's wrong. I'm scared I'm losing you.'

She looks down at him. At the broad plank of his back, the dark hairs on his neck. The secret synapses zapping in his head. All she can know about her husband is what he tells her or demonstrates. Knowing him is an act of faith, a decision to apply a set of ideas suggested by him and to believe in them. What else is knowing a person? Particularly a polite, caring man. They are attached. He loves her. It is a legal bond; she belongs to this marriage. It is an edifice they must maintain. He will not shirk his load; neither must she. She must bear it; brace herself. Dig in her heels. There is a way. She has no choice. She is feeble, lacking in the small amount of moral fibre to do what really OUGHT to be done. But she doesn't even dare think what that is. She reaches out, her hand hovers over his head, riding on the haze of energy around his body. Her scalp is numb; she is drunk. Cora strokes his soft hair. He takes her hand and kisses the palm.

'I'll have a shower, but I'll come back down. OK? We could watch some TV together.' He nods, relieved.

She leaves the kitchen, and enters the hall, retrieving her bags. Outside, the dark is relieved by the moon; a couple of police officers, unsexed by their knife-proof vests, slowly walk by, their gait altered by their official boots. She walks up the stairs, her bags in one hand, the other hand resting on the banister, soft against the grain of the polished wood. There is no way forwards or back. She must learn to stay put.

She reaches the bedroom before she realises he has followed. She moves around the platform of the bed to the safety of her side of the room. Where her things are placed, her nightstand with clock, contraceptives, hand-cream and lamp. Where a pile of books waits to be read, like sand bags piled up to protect her from his attentions. She reads to while away the moments until he is safely asleep. Not seeing the words. Remote, like snow or sunlight or flowers. She switches on her lamp and drops the bag into the drawer just in time. He pushes open the door, contrite but pleased with himself.

'You don't mind? I thought I'd join you.' He smiles, exposing his teeth. His shirt is undone at the neck, the hollow at the base of his throat pulses. He moves towards her, around the bed. She sits, removing her shoes, blocking him. It's too hot. She knows that he wanted her to stand waiting for him, face upturned, ready for his arms to fold around her. For him to kiss her. That was what she ought to have done. She missed the choreography. She is out of step with the chorus. He stops by her side, fumbling at her back for the fastening of her dress. Leaning over her, his breath assaulting her cheek. She continues to remove her shoes. Placing each ugly bare foot on the carpet.

'I can do it.' She reaches up and unzips her dress. Lifting it up and over her head. He stands next to her, not touching, unsure what he should do next.

'I thought I'd come in the shower with you. Soap your body and wash your hair. You know, be close to you. Would you like that?'

'I'm really tired. I just want a quick wash. Then I'll come down and join you. OK? Maybe another day.'

He resists. He is in love. He is in love with her loose skin, her sagging breasts, her scar tissue. He desires her. She is young, still in her thirties. He wants to deposit his love inside her. Remind her of old pleasures. His body signals his love. He wants to reach inside her and feast on her organs. Gorge himself on her inner workings. He is in love with her.

'Let me pleasure you. I'll do anything you want. Let me spoil you, darling.'

'No. Honestly, I just want to be alone for a minute. I want a shower and I want to relax. I'm tired, I'm sorry. I know you are doing something nice for me and I'm sorry. I just need some peace for a minute. OK?'

They are sliced apart. The room intervenes. He backs away, moving towards the door.

'Of course, no problem. I'm sorry. I should just let you be for a moment. I didn't mean to be selfish...'

'I know, I wasn't...'

'It's fine, Cora. I understand.' He turns and leaves the room. She hears him hurry down the stairs, away from her. The TV is turned on, the hollow sounds of recorded laughter rise like heat through the floorboards. She takes the box from the drawer. Pulling her robe over her underwear she walks down the hall to the bathroom. She turns on the light and locks the door behind her. She must maintain the happy household. She reaches into the shower cubicle and turns on the water. A mirror reflects her movements. She turns to it, dropping her robe and removing her bra and knickers. The light is harsh, clinical. The room shifts position. The machinery of her eye readjusts. A trick of the light, you can't believe what your eyes tell you. She watches herself. Her rib cage rising and falling.

Opening the box, her hand steady. A gift, a promise, lies within. A promise worth making can't be kept. But it's too late now. Twinned, her image in the mirror apes her gesture. She is doubled, split down the middle. She lifts out the small objects; they glint in the palm of her hand. The street outside is reduced to a muddle by the patterned glass in the window. Forced out of focus, nothing can be seen clearly, only the impression of a tree remains. She is isolated. In the middle of two opposing sides. She opens the mouth of one of the silver clamps and fits it over her nipple. With her forefinger and thumb she twists the tiny screw that draws the bars on either side closed. It lays flat against her skin, unobtrusive except for the bulging breast tissue. She fits the other one.

The water runs behind her, steam unfolds and condenses on the cold mirror. She disappears from view. She tightens the screws, making the necessary adjustments, fixing the machine. She steps into the shower, the water hot on her head, running into her eyes. Blinded, she can feel everything. She is an animal, feeling nothing more than physical sensation. She is annulled by the pain that threads through her. She is wiped out. She tightens the clamps even more. Her breasts burn, her blood races through her system, she is finely tuned. Suffering, unthinking, comprised only of sensation. She suffers, offering her pain to the water that washes it down into the sewage. She is water, air, mass. She is the sea. Salty and poisonous. She is alive, a sea sponge, without a nervous, digestive or circulatory system. The water possesses her, feeds her, nurtures her. It flows through her, unchanged. Laughter penetrates the bathroom from downstairs. Her relief flows through the cracks. She is released and gulps air. Blameless, she is a configuration of cells that mutates and replicates. She is what nature made her.

Stepping from the shower, she wraps the towel around her body. The clamps pinch her skin, innocent as history. She undoes them, slowly, reversing the pressure. Purple bruises ring her nipples. She drops the clamps into her pocket, wraps her hair in a towel. Freshly washed, she is purified. Newly punished, she has paid her debt.

I like driving, especially at night. Feeling safe in a warm, enclosed capsule, other cars and drivers reduced to nothing more than the rapid approach and then fading away of light. Music on, blocking out all other sounds. I hold the steering wheel and feel powerful and competent. I love this car. We're free and safe. My fingers curled around the smooth leather, following the road. Clearly defined, practical. Everything within reach and perfectly designed. I like the thunk of the door closing and the click of the seat belts. The immensely satisfying sounds and smells of a good car. The kids asleep in the back seat, little heads too heavy for their necks, their chins on their chest, drooling. Dreaming their multi-coloured dreams, tired out after racing around all day, their faces sticky with sweat and sugar. And you next to me, quiet, sometimes handing me a mint or one of the kid's fruit sweets or reaching for the volume dial to turn the radio up. I glance over at you, your face in shadow, turned towards your window, unsure if you're asleep or not, I reach over and stroke your thigh, cup your knee. My thumb testing the texture of your skin. You take my hand, stroke it twice and move it from your leg.

You don't stir, you don't startle. You don't move. The children are stirring. I can hear Jessica talking to her teddy. I must keep all this to myself. This misery, this rage. How dare you? How fucking dare you? The children must be protected as best we can. How fucking dare you. This isn't just about us; it's about them, their future, their happiness. We were happy. We were so happy. Remember?

When we were first together, I did all the driving, you'd not got your licence then, you used to say 'what do I need to drive for, I've got you.' I liked driving you around. Waiting outside your flat, engine ticking over, watching you as you ran down the steps outside your door, your hair still damp, gloss on your lips. Smiling. You smiled for me that slow sweet smile, a cat-like smile, looking me straight in the eye, your brown eyes reflecting the orange light. You'd stretch out on the seat, putting your feet up on the dashboard, your skirt sliding down to your lap and I'd rest my hand on your skinny thighs. Sometimes we'd drive out of town with no particular place in mind, just driving, music on, you liked Daniel Johnston and would insist on playing the CD over and over. We'd drive out till we spotted something we liked, taking it in turns to pick a turning at a junction or a slip road off the motorway. We left things to chance, to serendipity. We trusted fate and ourselves; nothing fazed us then, getting lost and discovering something new was fun. We had time, time to waste. You smoking cigarettes with the window down, your tanned feet tapping out the tune and I would drive you, us.

All this before the children, when it was just me and you, freedom to roam and play, nothing to rush home for, no responsibilities. Sometimes we'd end up in a village pub, drinking and laughing, chatting to the locals, playing darts badly and eating ploughman's lunches with sweaty cheddar and limp salad. Once we spotted a field full of wild flowers, poppies and ox-eye daisies and vetch, so we parked on the verge and wandered into the middle of the field to eat our picnic of cheap wine and Cornish pasties that we'd bought in the garage. Surrounded by the flowers and long grass, we made love, with you giggling that you had ants in your pants while the grass tickled my balls.

There was that time when we stopped in Margate, a desolate little seaside town that you said Turner had stayed and painted in. You'd had summer holidays there as a little girl, camping with your parents. You pointed out where the Crazy Golf had been on the pier and the area of the beach where the donkeys had waited for their sharp-heeled passengers. You ate a pink and white ice cream and we bought tickets for the rundown amusement park and rode the loop-the-loop roller coaster, I screamed and you smiled while I was sick after.

Then there was the time we drove to a church with Chagall windows. All blues and purples, the crucified Christ looking as if he were caught up in waves or a tumbling sky. I remember being embarrassed, because I wanted you to be impressed by my artistic flair and understanding and of course I have very little and had still less then. I talked and talked and wanted to say the right thing and you walked around, quietly looking, saying nothing much. I tried so hard to be profound. You were too polite to tell me to be quiet. The windows were a memorial for a girl drowned at sea, someone's daughter. You told me you thought the time was right to try for a baby, you said in fact, 'I'd love a baby, let's make babies.' I said, 'One day we will.' But I wanted to keep you all to myself, keep our perfect life together unscathed. I never imagined I could love our children the way I do now. Now.

I try to think of these things slowly, detail by detail. The light in your hair, the cool flagstones, the curve of your neck, the hard wooden seats. The names carved into stone, the blue glass, brass candlesticks. The embroidered prayer cushions for devout knees. The smell of you. The feel of your hand in mine. I want to hold on to these images. I want to push back the growing fear, the hatred. I want to think only of when you were mine. Only mine. I'm getting old and bitter. Soon I won't recognise myself. You and the children are all I have. You are all I am.

This is a story of you I'm telling. Of us. That's all we are, stories, stories within stories, that overlap and link us together. I try to know you, but all I can know is the tale you tell and the tale I tell and perhaps that's all there is. A mess of stories that confuse and make no sense. How can two people be so happy together and end up like this? Weren't we better than this? This fucking obvious cliché? I am a man hanging by his fingertips, desperately alive, more alive because I know I will have to let go. Of you, of the kids. I will have to fall eventually. Knowing I'm about to lose everything makes it all so much more precious. That's another bloody cliché. Do you ever think like that? What are you afraid of? What would tear your world apart? Losing me? Him? The kids? You seem immune from loss. You move about the house like a ghost, as if I were watching a projection of you on a screen. Untouchable, just a trick of the light.

The morning reveals no visible change. Cora is alone with the children. He has left; his busy world of power and work demands his presence at 8:30 am sharp. She woke hopeful. The light pretending to differentiate between one day and the next. Night then day. Off/on. A new beginning, a genesis. The gift of forgetting and a remade past. She dressed herself first. Wearing the clamps under her bra. Conscientious reminders not to falter, as they do not falter with their biting presence. This is her day off: a part-timer, she is a part-time mother, worker and wife. He manages full-time everything. She is duly apportioned. Segmented: like a worm, each severed part can work autonomously.

Dressed and fed, the children sit in front of the TV. She has put cartoons on for them. They are mesmerised by the bright colours. She stands in the kitchen, her hands hanging limp in the sink, up to the wrists in hot water. She repents. So far, so good. Her flesh reminds her of her responsibility. The children are safe, clean, fed. She has almost completed the morning's tasks. Tick, tick, tick. She is washing the breakfast things – tick. She has made their packed lunches – tick. There is only the sound of the TV, which means they aren't fighting – tick. She is succeeding. Every movement of her arms pulls on her breasts, inflicting a fresh reminder. It perfects her. She reaches up to the cupboard to put the cereal bowls away. She is grateful.

Time to go. She calls them and they come quickly. Everything is under control. She tells them to get their shoes on. Jessica begins to cry that she can't put her shoes on by herself yet. Cora has transcended the details. She breathes. She is alive. The urge to slap the child silent is curbed by the vicious reminders she wears under her clothes. She bends at the knee and looks the child in the eye. I will help you. The girl sits at her mother's feet, extending her tiny legs. Cora cups the heel in her hand

and slides the black leather shoe onto Jessica's foot. She closes the buckle and repeats the same movement for the other foot. Cora stands and helps the child to her feet. Patrick waits for them. Able to tie his own laces, he is triumphantly independent.

Cora fetches her bag and her keys. She's decided they'll walk today. They leave the house, shutting the door behind them. The street is busy with school children, on foot and in cars. Children being shepherded to their classrooms by parents and nannies. The streets belong to the children for the next thirty minutes before they are banished and the women take over, along with the very young and the very old. Uniform houses line the road. Only the front doors differ. It promises to be a hot summer's day. The council have cleaned the streets; everything is in order.

The children with their small feet and short legs can take only very small steps. She strides ahead of them. They dawdle behind her. She waits for them to catch up. As soon as they do, she begins again walking at full pace; the children have to run to keep up with her. She takes their hands in hers. They cling to her, running alongside her. Jessica falters, tripping over her own feet: the only thing saving her from falling to her knees is her mother's grip. Cora feels the snap of impatience and yanks at the child's arm the way one would a dog's leash, delivering a sharp reprimand. The child yelps and Cora yanks again, the child momentarily suspended in the air, dangling from her mother's arm. Cora's own pain bites and she repents. She repents.

The pace she keeps maintains the pressure on her breasts. The soothing pangs bring her back to herself. Atonement. She tugs the children along, a flotilla of weeping little humans. The boy lags, is already tired before he has even got to school. He scuffs a shoe. Cora ignores him. They will succeed. They are already at least a third of the way to Jessica's nursery. They stop at the side of the road, waiting to cross. Looking and listening. Cora closes her hands tighter around the children's. To keep them safe. They step out into the road, crossing carefully. She is diligent. They get to the other side. Not much further. Patrick asks if they can slow down. She tightens her grip, feeling the tiny bones under their covering of skin. She is reminded of being taught to bone quail by her father. It was one Christmas, she thinks, years ago.

If they stop for even one moment she knows they will become distracted. Small children can find the strangest things interesting. The day elongates, spreads over specious measurements like minutes and hours, is viscous like a thickened fluid. The short journey drags. A cat sits on a garden wall, its tail twitching. The children stretch towards it, hands ready to stroke its soft fur. Overflowing with love and a need to possess, to clutch and squeeze, to love it to death, the children attempt to steer her towards the kitty. Cora marches on. Jessica whines at the end of her arm, dangling like an ornament. The pincers on Cora's flesh prompt her to remain calm. She is calm. She is doing very well.

Her pulse beats a new measurement. Quickened, everything around her is too slow, dull, pulling her back. She is adorned with a brand new humanity. She is remade, absolved. Jessica's nursery is thirty paces away. They are nearly there. Intact, the children are fine. These are new gestures, only the footsteps repeat, otherwise there is novelty; usually they take the car. This walking is brand new. Cora is confident she can manage change. She can make a choice. They turn through the gate into the small garden in front of the nursery. Bright clowns dance across the window. Letters of the alphabet line the windowsill. Cora rings the bell. Security is tight, guarding the precious little creatures. They are completely safe here amongst the professionally trained, carefully vetted and monitored staff.

A young woman dressed in a blue overall opens the door.

'Jessicat! Hello!' Her voice is as bright as the primary colours on the walls. She sweeps the little girl in, smiling at Cora. 'Could you sign the register please, Mum.' She directs Cora to the book open on a side table. 'Say bye, bye to Mummy, Jessicat!' The woman dials a code into the keypad next to a second set of security doors, waits for the discreet click of the lock and pushes the door open. With an energetic wave she and Jessica enter the nursery. Silenced, Cora shrinks from the woman's ease and authority over her child. The child even has a special name here. Cora signs her daughter over to them.

She and Patrick join the parade of other mothers and children moving towards his school. The building is new, low-built, hunkered close to the ground like an animal taking cover. It too announces its love of children with bright colours and pictures of flowers, animals and smiling faces. Cora is exhausted by the amount of loving required of her. She makes a final effort to maintain her composure. Patrick begins to pull at her hand. He has spotted his friends in the playground. She holds him tighter and tighter. Women gather around the gate ahead, talking and laughing. They are friends to one another. Their children the common subject, and of course husbands, boyfriends, homes, illnesses, food and jobs.

The boy pulls harder against her; she doesn't yield. A row of large black birds perch on a lamppost ahead of them, Cora is unsure whether they are crows or jackdaws or rooks. They maintain their mystery for her, unnamed. 'Look' she says pointing to the birds, 'they will peck out your eyes if you carry on being naughty.' Her son looks up at her, stunned. His eyes widen at the threat, increasing his vulnerability. Fear smothers him; he checks himself and keeps pace next to her. Looking down, he half closes his eyes, just in case. She is in control. Thrilled. She is pleased by his fear. It reassures her as completely as money in the bank. The morning is nearly over. They are almost there.

They are so close she can hear the conversations emanating from the huddle of mothers. She looks ahead, not meeting anyone's eye. She can imagine what they say about her when her back is turned. Odd, stuck up, a bitch, who does she think she is, not one of us. She knows exactly what they say and she cares deeply. She wants to belong with them. She would like to be invited into the huddle, to go to the coffee mornings and the PTA meetings. She raises her free hand to her hair and shakes herself loose from the desire to be their friend. What good would it do?

Patrick tugs violently against her hand. Cora looks down at him. Tears fill his eyes, his hand clamped over his mouth trying to muffle a sob. He has stepped in dog shit. The filth covers his black leather shoe and oozes onto his sock. Cora attempts to breathe, the stench filling her mouth. Her ears ring. The boy shrinks from her.

'I'm sorry, Mummy, I'm sorry.'

She drags him harder by the arm towards the school 'How did you manage that you stupid, stupid little boy?' She drags him past the tutting women gathered round the gate, and up the path. 'I'll have to clean you off now, you fucking twerp. For God's sake, couldn't you watch where you were going for a fucking second?' Another woman steps aside allowing them past, her face wide open with shock.

Cora is controlled by her violence. It twists her limbs, contorts her face. Her lip curls around the words she wants to shove down his throat. She wants to punish him. Beat him with her fists for wasting her time, for not taking care. She gives him a shake, as much as she can muster in public, 'What do you say?'

'Sorry, Mummy. I'm so sorry, Mummy.' He is crying openly now, not bothered by the audience of other small boys watching him act like a baby. What a baby! Mummy's boy! He stands in a puddle of her poison. She pulls him again, his arm numb and edging out of its socket. A fraction more and she'll pull it free, leave it hanging useless from his shoulder. What would his father say? They enter the school building. She is unstoppable.

A staff member approaches. 'Can I help you? It isn't time to come in yet.'

Cora points to the boy's shoe. 'I need to clean him up before school starts.'

'Ah, OK. The boys' toilets are just down there. You could use some tissue and water.'

Mother and son walk together in step for the first time towards the lavatories. He walks the shit through the building, leaving honest footprints. They pass through a corridor lined proudly with the splodges and scribbles produced by the barely literate children. Despite the restraint of the clamps, her temper rages. They leave a trail of muck. The boys' toilets open off the corridor to the right. White tiles with dirty grouting line the room. It stinks from years' worth of accidents from clumsy little boys and their haphazard penises. The cubicles are only chest height to Cora; the lavatories are tiny miniaturised versions. Even the sinks are lower..

'Take your shoe off and give it to me.' She tears a fistful of toilet paper from a roll and reaches for the shoe. Patrick continues to sob. His pale hand covered in shit as he undoes his shoelace.

'And your sock, Stupid.' She holds the shoe under a tap and scrubs at it with the paper. The paper disintegrates and the shit is smeared further into the shoe. 'Jesus Christ.' Cora can taste her hatred, thick and delicious. She is tired of fighting against it. Its bright tang coats her tongue, slides down her throat. It fills her belly, she feels contented at last. Satisfied. She scrubs at the shoe, cleaning it. It is soaking wet, as is the sock. She is tempted to smear the shit over the walls, over the boy's face and body. She stops herself. Her anger is intoxicating. It pushes for more, hungers for more hatred. She hands him the sopping sock, 'Put that on.'

'But Mummy it's wet.' He looks up at her, his nose red, eyelashes stuck together in spikes by his tears, pitifully dishevelled by her violence. He shivers as he stands there with one bare foot.

'Tough. Maybe next time you'll watch where you are going.' She watches him struggle to pull on the sock, hampered by his trembling and the wet fabric. 'Hurry up! What is wrong with you?' Outside the room she can hear the sounds of the new school day. Hundreds of little feet run towards classrooms, giggling and whispering. She rips the sock from his hand and pushes him to the floor; he crashes onto his backside, hitting his head against the wall. 'Don't you dare cry.' She drags the sock onto his foot, bending back his toes. 'There, not so difficult was it?' His confusion blights his ability to answer. He doesn't recognise her. He knows a cool, controlled mother. One who does her duty, who conforms. This one is ill-disciplined. This one is a bad mummy. This one is brand new.

The door to the room opens just as she is forcing his sodden shoe onto his foot. The headmistress, young, well-dressed, patient, pops her head elegantly around the doorframe.

'Oh dear! Have we had an accident?'

Cora pushes the boy towards the woman. 'He'll be fine. He stood in dog dirt on our way here.' Cora stands straight, handing the child over to their better care for the rest of the day. She looks down at him, his tear-marked face, authentic and proofed, watermarked; his one wet foot, his messy hair. The hatred wavers for a moment.

'Ah! Accidents happen, no need for tears!' The woman cajoles with a wave of her hand, she performs her act for them. She is calm, wise and an expert with children. She has qualifications to prove it. Years of training and experience all rolled up into her degree. Patrick doesn't look at Cora, only mumbles goodbye when prompted by his teacher. Together the woman and the boy leave, her gentle hand on his shoulder, guiding him as he leaves alternate wet footprints.

It is only when she is halfway home that she realises what she has done. When time reconnects with her senses. She is uncontrollable. Everything she knew she could be, she has become. This is not the careful scraping towards a happy ending. She is not the smiling face at the end of a careful accumulation of triumphs. She moves forwards, monstrous. She remembers the look on the other mothers' faces as she left the school. What she is, is now out in the open. It can't be hidden or excused. Like all criminals, the bad come to light in the end. She is the one rotten apple that can make the barrel bad. She must be sought out. She must be stopped. She is what normal people despise. A mother who shoves and pushes her own child, she is sick, against nature.

She walks home, slowly. She can no longer supersede the minutes and seconds of human measurement. The pain in her chest is gone. She is used to it; become accustomed. The metal additions belong on her body now. She is once again unfeeling. She swings her legs from side to side, unable to walk properly. Detached from her brain, a dead thing. She begins to cry. The boy's fear penetrates her. She wonders if he will forget. If he will begin the afternoon with a clean slate. All children are chastised, shouted at, told off. What's different about this? Perhaps he won't remember her hatred, her enjoyment of his fear. She has dwindled to nothing. She must run. Get off the street.

The key slides into the lock. The door opens easily. There is no trickery. The postman has been. Bills and catalogues litter the mat. She bends to pick them up, walks with them in her hand through to the kitchen and places them neatly on the counter for her husband. Summer is over. The catalogues have models in winter clothing on the covers. Time passes. She performs the correct duties. The children are safely at school. All is OK. She is not what she once was. She changes. She has changed, continues to change. She longs for permanence. Standing in the shit of her shame she behaves like her old self. She flicks on the kettle for tea. She turns on an appliance. She begins to put away the clean crockery from breakfast. She repeats. She performs. She slides about the kitchen on putrid rotting limbs. She is the sickness in the house.

The boy will forget today. He is six; today will fade into the happy pile of Christmas, birthday and holiday memories. She cannot forget. She has failed. She undoes her shirt and reaches into the cups of her bra. The clamps grip her in silent contemplation. She is too much for them. She pulls them off without loosening them. No real harm done. Flesh does not resist. It obeys. She will be better. She will find a way. She will learn to show love. She will learn patience and kindness. She will teach herself and if that doesn't work she will be taught. She drops the clamps in the bin. They clang against the metal, tolling like a bell just once as they land.

It is all unnecessary. She could pack a bag and leave. She could up and go. That is possible. She could do what men do and turn tail and run. Not think twice. She could hide in a bed-sit and work as a barmaid. She could fuck strangers for fun. She could travel the world. See the sights. He would marry again, a lovely kind woman who would love the children. Who might have some of her own. They could have more together, increasing the joy, doubling the brood. She could travel light, free as a bird, but always scarred, never able to deny their existence. Her body would always mother them. The two children. Her eggs, his fluids. The transformation. The unbearable explosion of her belly. She would never be able to deny them. No matter how far she went. Worse, they would come looking for her. She would be hunted, a fugitive from maternal duty.

She folds a tea towel. The light is beautiful in the kitchen at this time of day. She stirs sugar into her cup. Milk. She sits at the table, the cup between her hands. The wounded finger has begun to heal. She feels no pain. The body is miraculous in its ability to mend itself. Soon she will almost be intact again. Only small marks will remain. Small reminders. History recorded on the body. Her body is a text. She still smells of dog shit from earlier. She will never forget what she is. She must be punished.

I'm jealous of Patch. My own son. The way you look at him, hold him. I am jealous of Patrick. There. That's my guilty secret. I hide it and I live with it and I know it's immature and I love him. I love his sticky little hands, and his bright little smile. I love the way he rakes through his Lego as if it were a percussive instrument when I'm trying to watch TV and the way he curls in my lap for a cuddle. I sometimes just stand outside his bedroom door listening to him playing with his toys; to the conversations he has with his imaginary friends and the battles he sets up with his toy soldiers. You see, I do love him. He is my boy, my son, and yet...

I envy your relationship with him. I envy the easy closeness you have, the intimacy. Your love for him. Everyone knows a mother and son have an infrangible bond. It began of course when you were pregnant with him, before he even really existed. Except of course, that he did exist for you, he was absolutely present for you, but for me he was entirely abstract. A pulsating mound in your belly. The two of you tied together as one. You feeling his kicks first, his somersaults. I know you said it hurt and that you didn't like it, but I think you only said that to make me feel better. To include me in some small way. So that we'd take sides together. You said it was like carrying a battering ram inside you. I appreciated that you tried to draw me in, to share the experience, but I was completely shut out. Your body was no longer about the two of us. It was about the two of you. Then you began to close down. I felt the shift of your love from me to him and then of course to Jessica. I don't regret the kids. God no. I can't imagine life without them. I just wish that I still mattered, that there was enough space for me. Too late. It can't be too late. I want you to see me again. I don't want to be just an extension of the children. Their father.

I remember walking into our bedroom, we were still in the flat then, we moved when Patch was two, didn't we? And you were standing in front of the mirrored wardrobes in just your knickers, crying. More than crying, you said you couldn't take it anymore. You'd been watching him move under your skin. You thought you looked ugly but you didn't. You were beautiful, I know that, all pregnant women are beautiful: it's one of those clichés that happens to be absolutely true. You hated that your breasts rested on your stomach and that you couldn't reach down to tie your shoes. You hated not being able to sleep; you said it frightened you feeling him move, autonomous, inside you. That you felt possessed by a demon, just silly hormonal talk I thought and I told you so. You needed to be treated gently and with patience, my own father had warned me about that, in fact all the books you'd bought and read from cover to cover had pretty much said the same thing. That you must be cared for and watched tenderly. And I did my best.

My sister said that it's hard to predict just how a woman will respond to the challenges of pregnancy, but most love it, all get over it. I knew that deep down you would be fine. That mother nature would step in and you would blossom. And you suited your face looking rounder, you had hips and tits. You were really sexy. I wanted you more than ever, though I understood you needed to be left alone, I guess that didn't help how I felt though, pushed out, rejected. In all these things, there is no room for a man, for the father. Your job is done except for fetching and carrying. Other women close ranks around the new mother, it is entirely esoteric, unfathomable. My mother and sister fussed around you, sending you vitamins and support tights and all these other strange things that a man can't even begin to imagine you might need. Your mother knitted tiny clothes with antique names, booties, bonnets and matinee jackets. Your friends bought you special foods and magazines and body lotions and brightly coloured babygrows that were impossible to fasten properly. I was taken by complete surprise by it all. By its complexity. How could something so natural, so animal, be so difficult, require so much equipment?

You were this private space, a walking intimate zone of just you and him. You had to eat certain things, sleep at certain times, he kicked you so much you had heartburn and piles and your breasts changed size and shape and colour and your hair got thicker and you even smelt different; everything changed. Everything. And I was so sure I'd be a great father and a good husband, I thought I would be great at it, but how could I be when I resented my own child. I was scared and ashamed, with no one to talk to. Sometimes I'm so lonely and you're right there in the room with me. But I can't tell you this. How can I tell you all this? You'd leave me and take the children and then I'd be nothing.

Then you went into labour with a trickle of water like you were peeing yourself. I'd imagined a great gush and then pandemonium and drama. I didn't expect the slow, agonising wait, of going back and forth to the hospital while your body slowly opened up to let him out. The packing and repacking of your bag, with baby clothes and sandwiches and ice water and nipple cream, scented candles, CDs, a TENS machine with tangled wires and sticky pads and on and on with all these things that myriad experts told us we'd need. Things that the pile of magazines and books that sat by our sofa had decreed were absolutely essential to a balanced, joyful birth, which was essential to a healthy, happy baby. Our lives were being directed by all these so-called experts, but where did we fit in? Where did I fit in? Where was the promised joy?

That final day, when you were taken in after three days of the back and forth, they hooked you up to a monitor and the small birthing room was filled with the strange metallic beeps of Patch's heartbeat, while a machine scratched out the rise and fall on a long sheet of paper. It was taking too long. You tried a warm bath; you sat on a huge bouncy ball and circled your hips.

You stood up and leant against me, moaning. And you cried and cried. You refused drugs, no gas and air, no injection, nothing.

Nothing I said or did helped. It was as if you didn't see or hear anyone, you were so far sunk down inside yourself. I was the intruder. I had no place there in that shabby room. You had the midwife and the doctor; you didn't need me. Eventually they made you lie down on the bed and put your feet in the stirrups. They gathered between your legs, dressed in their strange blue outfits and stood watching as you tried to push him out. You strained so hard a blood vessel in your eye burst and you looked like you'd been punched for days after. Then finally the doctor eased the huge metal forceps inside you and pulled that blue-skinned little creature out as you screamed. Patrick. And I loved him on sight. I loved him so much it almost hurt. You were exhausted, so they wrapped him up and handed him to me. There was blood and fluid everywhere. It was like a battlefield. No one prepares you for how violent it all is or how shocking. I've caught and killed and skinned rabbits but nothing prepares you for the gore of childbirth.

But in my arms was this damp little thing, looking barely human, his face all squashed and smelling oddly of you and blood. Our son. I thought everything would be all right from that moment. They stitched you up, your poor body, while I cradled him, you too tired to even look at him for very long. He lay there in my arms, snuffling, his tiny face screwed up against the light. His very first moments in the world, just lying there, in my arms, breathing. I was so proud of you both.

The weeks following zipped by so fast; the flat was teeming with visitors and flowers and balloons. They drank champagne brought over by my father; I drank sparkling water with you, so you didn't feel left out. Both our mothers seemed to be permanently with us, washing something or making tea. You sat serenely in the middle of it all, Patch in his cradle next to you, mewling for milk. Everyone said what a good baby he was, sleeping so much so early. He looked just like me, even then, though I think he has your personality, your quiet self-possession. Sometimes I catch the two of you, staring ahead, daydreaming, with exactly the same expression on your faces. We were never alone those first weeks. It was relentlessly busy. Then suddenly they were all gone, Patch had become just a normal part of our life, and we were left to cope.

I'd go out to work in the morning after kissing you both and return later to find you both still in the same clothes and the flat smelling of sour milk and baby shit. It sounds awful, but I remember it as being a blissful chaos, baby clothes and discarded nipple pads, muslins crusted with milk and baby sick everywhere. I would clean the kitchen before putting one of mum's frozen meals in the microwave for our dinner. I bought you flowers and a diamond pendant because someone in the office told me it was tradition to buy your wife a diamond after every baby. I never minded the expense. I imagined that you needed me, that cleaning and cooking connected me to the two of you – the two of you in your blissful, crooning bubble. I belonged with the two of you.

Motherhood changed you. Not just in the obvious ways, but something unseen. I would watch you feeding Patch, his clean little mouth sucking on your breast and you made a circle together. It was a continuation of the isolation of pregnancy, you only existed for each other, and nothing else was real for you. You would stare into space, lost in thought as you detached him, tucked your breast back into the feeding bra and switched sides, exposing the other breast and bringing the baby to it, it all seemed so natural to you, as if you did it on autopilot. You belonged together. It was like watching an animal, where everything is instinctive, nothing learnt. I said that to you once, remember? And you laughed at me; you said 'I had to learn. I had no idea what was expected of me, what the child would want. I had to learn.' That was a surprise to me. The way you were, I didn't imagine there was any learning involved. It's gotten easier, I was able to get more involved with him, he began to walk and talk and play and then Jessica came along. I began to belong to them, they began to reach out to me, call for me, were soothed when I picked them up; those sort of things, I love playing with them, listening to them as they chatter away. Holding their little bodies close, making them laugh. They are my life. I do my best to be a good father and husband, but still you never came back to me. Our family's complete: you, me, our two beautiful children, and nothing has been the same since.

She felt like she'd been beaten up. Done ten rounds with Mike Tyson. Her whole body soured by pain.

The head, the heaviest part, was cradled in the nook of her elbow. The predictable trajectory of light sliced through the peace in the little room, the blue light binding; without it they wouldn't exist. Her back ached. Warmed air was pumped from vents around the room, a careful temperature to ease and comfort. She was too hot, damp under her arms, her cheeks a pinched red. The baby, a perfect mouth encircling her nipple, like a snare, reached tiny fingers to her breast and clawed at the soft flesh; its translucent fingernails sharp. Its hunger drove an infant violence, like a kitten, a scrap of cute death, the child struggled, its legs drawn up in protest. It gulped, its tongue scraping at the nipple forcing a bloom of milk, the binding flow, but also the firm suck brought blood, a blister. She was completed, reduced. Shrunk to this flow. This pain.

It gorged, first one breast then the next and when finished, belched up the excess, including a spot of her blood, trickling from the corner of its mouth. Its unfocused eyes blinked, lizard-like, and it curled up on itself and slept. Her breasts, heavy with milk, leaked droplets of pale thin liquid; she wondered how such pallid looking fluid could nourish anything. She cupped them in her hands, taking the weight for a moment, she didn't recognise them, large and blue-veined with the nipple grown bigger and darker. She didn't recognise herself.

Her body colossal with its new role, wounded and tentative, she moved carefully. Her hands, restrained by nervousness and fear, folded tiny woollen items into quarters and put them away in her bag. Home soon. Perhaps the next day. She sucked in breath through her open mouth. Everything would be fine. The baby was neat in his transparent crib. Drab towelling encased the fragile weave of his flesh; he was clean and tidy, perfumed and scrubbed by the capable nurses. Cora had watched them bathe the baby, tucked like a parcel under the nurse's arm, his papier-mâché thin head cupped in the palm of her hand. The nurse tested the temperature of the water with her elbow and then washed the baby's head, careful around the pulsing gap in his skull. All the while talking, explaining, soothing. Not once flicking a drop of water in the baby's face. She immersed his body in the water, supporting his head. The baby completely safe and relaxed.

'Ah! A water baby!' the nurse said. 'What a precious little man!'

Later when Cora tried to bathe the child he screamed and thrashed his arms even though she did her best to replicate the nurse. She gave up and wrapped him in a towel and laid him on the bed, away from harm. When her husband visited the baby snuffled, fed, and delighted with his clucks and coos, pursed lips and involuntary frowns. Her husband filled the tiny room with his pride, holding his son to his chest, smiling shiny-eyed at Cora. Nurses moved in and out of the room at hourly intervals, taking measurements, checking rhythms, outputs, inputs, encouraging sleep, encouraging gentle exercise, encouraging. Checking up on her. Perhaps she can't be trusted? Cora wondered. Is she getting this wrong?

The shocking red oval of the baby's cry flung itself around the room, against the sealed windows like a trapped bird. But mostly he slept and the room vibrated with his unrehearsed breaths as she watched him, unsure what else was required.

When other babies cried, their wails drifting in from the ward outside their room, she was unmoved. But her child's cry seemed to penetrate to the core of her self, controlling her, moving her limbs and setting the pace of her heart. Instinct has keen senses. The nights had changed, like lovers she and the child were getting used to their relationship, gazing at each other. No longer blurred by wine or sleep concealed, the night was sharp-edged in her wakefulness, with the child stirring needing to be fed. Its mouth closing around anything offered, the tiny jaw working back and forth.

Finally, she got dressed; the maternity clothes loose over her smaller self. She pulled them on carefully over bruises the colour of oil. The baby, distinct and separate, no longer a part of her, no longer just hers to experience. She was empty, rejected by the child in its quest for life, shrugged off like an overcoat in a hot room. What had been an idea was now real, finite, able to die. She feared the baby's inevitable death, even though it was likely she would be dead herself and oblivious, but still she couldn't stand the idea. Everyone congratulated her on the new life she had brought into the world, but all she could think was that she had given birth to the potential for death. She leant over the sleeping form and felt for breath with the back of her hand. So tired... she longed for sleep. The feelings would come soon enough. When she had slept. Then the love she'd been told about would overwhelm her and everything would finally be alright.

Her parents visited, with flowers they weren't allowed to leave in case of infection. Her mother picked up the baby, her deft hand sliding under his head and supporting his whole body. Her father peered over his wife's shoulder gazing at his grandson.

'Look at him! What an angel. He's got my nose, hahaha! He's got his granddad's nose! Well, look at that. Haven't you done well?' He turned to Cora, smiling, his eyebrows raised up like knots beneath his hairline. 'He's perfect. I'm so proud of you both.'

Her mother cooed and sang to the baby, whose blank blue eyes stared up at her.

'How're you feeling?'

'Awful. Why doesn't anyone tell you how bad it is?'

Her father laughed, 'Because then no one would have babies.'

'Well, it might minimize the shock. Just to know what to expect.'

'Nonsense, silly girl. Millions of women have babies every day and they do just fine and then go and do it all over again, some of them having their babies squatting in a field all on their own.'

'Don't exaggerate, Mary. Squatting in a field. Bloody hell.'

'I just want her to realize how lucky she is. Nice room all to herself, nurses and everything and look at this darling little angel. So precious.' Her mother nuzzles the baby's nose with her own, breathing in his scent. 'It's such a wonderful time, Cora. Treasure every moment, they grow so fast, you won't know where the time went.' The baby slept on, wrapped in his blue blanket.

Once, years ago, when winter was finally giving in to spring, she'd been surrounded by a ring of girls. They stood around her, shoulder to shoulder in their blue grammar school blazers. Thick make-up around their eyes; their knees exposed by their skirts.

'Excuse me, please,' she'd said, trying to elbow her way out of the circle.

'Listen to her! "Scuse me please!"' The ringleader was a pudgy girl with bright red curls hanging over her left eye, the rest of her hair shaved at the back and sides and a fringe of heavy gold earrings that traced the curl of her ear. 'What's your name then?'

'Cora.' She tried to stand up straight, shifting her bag onto her shoulder. Her sock sagged around her ankle and for a moment she wondered about whether to pull it up or not. She decided not.

'Cora. Cora. What sort of a fucking name is that?' The others laughed at the pudgy girl's wit.

'You go to St. John Fisher's, right? The whorehouse on the hill. You a whore, Cora?'

'No. I'm not. Why are you?'

'Feisty, ain't it?' said a short blonde to Cora's right.

'Just fuck off.'

'Listen to it! Oh my god! What a cheek. Be polite, Cora. It's not nice to swear, is it?' A tall girl with dyed black hair chipped in, glancing over at the pudgy girl, looking for approval. The pudgy girl laughed, followed by the others.

'I don't want any trouble, I just want to go home.' Cora had never been in a fight before. Her heart shook in her chest, her blouse stuck to her sweaty skin. She shivered despite being too hot in her blazer. She tried to swallow but she felt sick, as if her stomach had turned itself inside out.

'What – to your mummy and daddy? Are they waiting for their ickle baby?'

'Maybe. So what?'

'Mouthy for someone who don't want trouble, ain't ya? I like your shoes. Let's have a look.' Pudgy girl pointed down to Cora's feet, at her navy blue Kickers.

Cora stood square on her feet.

'You a rich girl then? Mummy and Daddy got lots of money?'

'Must be to have a pair of them,' said the tall girl.

'What size are you?' asked Pudgy.

Cora said nothing, looking through them. It had to be over soon. It had to.

'I reckon she's a size 5, same as me. Give us your shoes. Come on, I asked nice.'

'No. Now let me go. Alright? Fuck off.' She pulled a breath in through her mouth.

'Come on then, if you think you're so tough, whore. Let's have it.' The pudgy one stepped forward, almost touching Cora.

'No, I'm not starting trouble. OK?'

The girls laughed, nudging each other as if she'd cracked the best joke they'd ever heard.

When the first punch connected with her cheek it was a relief: finally she knew precisely what was happening, the mystery, the dreadful anticipation of pain dissolved, leaving no trace of fear. She barely felt the push to the ground or the kick to her stomach; she was almost surprised to find herself lying on the pavement, her knee scraped raw and pink. She wasn't shaking or crying. She felt exhilarated.

An older woman pulling a plaid shopping trolley interrupted the fight. 'What on earth?'

The others sauntered off, laughing. 'See ya later, Cora-whora!'

'You OK, love?' The woman bent over Cora, reaching into her pocket for a handkerchief and offering it to her. 'Oh dear, you're going to have a shiner tomorrow I think.'

'I'm OK, thank you.' Cora stood, her legs unsteady. 'I'd best go home.'

'If you're sure? Alright then. Take care.' The woman tucked her hankie back into her pocket, looked Cora up and down and walked away, pulling her heavy trolley behind her.

Her father opened the front door to her. 'Bloody hell, what's happened to you?'

'Some girls beat me up, Dad.'

'Who? Which girls?'

'Girls from the grammar school.'

'Where the bloody hell did this happen.'

'Near the precinct. Opposite the football pitch.'

'Oh darling, let me have look at you.' He cupped her face in his hands and tilted it towards the light. 'They clumped you a good'un there, didn't they? They hit you anywhere else?'

'Not really. Just pushed me over. They wanted to take my boots.'

'Thieving little devils.' He brushed her hair back from her face. 'You'll live. I hope you hit them back.'

Cora shrugged.

'Does it hurt?'

She nodded and started to cry.

'Oh angel, don't cry. Daddy's here. Daddy will always be here. I love you and I always will. I won't let anyone hurt my little girl.' His hands firm around her waist. She was all light and air, delicate and protected, the pain hot and comforting in the pit of her chest. Alive. Her father stroked her back, smoothed her hair, his large fingers confirming her shape, the carpet burning a nylon heat into her feet. Behind them, sealed off behind the glass of the window, her mother stood in the rectangular garden, a rake in her left hand, the bright flare of pink delphiniums eclipsing her face.

The baby began to grizzle and cry, his tiny fists waving around his head.

'Someone needs a feed!' her mother said, bringing the baby over to her.

'Again? I've only just fed him.'

'Well, that's babies for you.' Her mother placed the infant in her arms, deft and expert.

Cora fumbled with the top of her nightgown, trying to unhook the feeding panel and keep hold of the baby.

'Here, let me do that. You'll see, you'll be able to do everything one-handed soon enough!' Her mother undid the button, exposing Cora's skin and the straps of the feeding bra. Her father averted his eyes, looking intently out of the window at the streets outside the hospital. Cora felt something between them slip. She was no longer daddy's little girl, but this little boy's mother. She turned the baby towards her breast and he latched on.

'Oh look at that. She's a natural.' Mary sighed, smiling to herself, her hands tucked inside one another.

Africa moves closer to Europe. The Continents slide over the soft mantle of the earth creating fissures and creases, tearing the ocean floor apart. The Mediterranean, now a holiday spot, was once a super ocean that girdled the earth and will eventually be remade as a mountain range. Imagine that. Geologists study the diaspora of sediments, scattered by the caravan of moving lands; grains of African rock are found deep in the core of South America; Britain is only separated from Europe by a temporary sea. Nothing is fixed, nothing.

You know at first this theory was denied by Russia and America, not wanting to believe their nations were in flux. That the land they claimed and fought so hard to protect was changing and shifting under their feet. It must have felt like a betrayal.

The sea rushes to fill the spaces. Tectonic plates shift, imperceptibly, beyond human notice, in deep time. As fast as a fingernail grows, the continents drift together. A new distribution of land and sea; allegiances will have to change. The history books won't make sense, knowledge will have to adjust. Think of it. Amazing. Molten magma will erupt from openings in the ground, like wounds, spewing hot coals into the air; decrepit volcanoes will collapse, there will be earthquakes and tidal waves that claw at the land. New weather systems will be created; hot air sent back and forth, clouds of ash and snow. The Poles will exchange their places, reorienting iron deposits in the soil. First North then South and back again. All the changes recorded and noted in layers of rock, waiting to be deciphered out in the open air. I wonder if Humanity will survive, if our descendants will still be around. Everything changes, you see? Even the fabric of the world.

Cora is sitting on a low banquette, her bare knees higher than her hips. She tries to sit elegantly, without showing her thighs, as she gulps her wine. She tugs at her skirt every few minutes to check it hasn't slipped up under her bottom. She is surrounded by some of the women from her office; she barely knows them except for Sonja, who sits to her right, her large bosom pressing against her low cut shirt. Sonja laughs loudly and often. Most of the women are younger than Cora, single, non-mothers. They wear a lot of make-up and carry expensive handbags. She imagines she is one of them, free and solid with her edges clearly defined. Utterly singular and without links or connections elsewhere, like a stone or an orphan or a collapsing star. Being with them purifies her, if only for a short while. She could almost be one of them, incapable of destruction.

They are in a bar, packed full of other city workers. Men and women shout to be heard over the music, the men have loosened their ties, their bags and briefcases are tucked away at their feet. Ropes of blue lights festoon the dark room. A long bar stretches along the wall behind which young bartenders in tight t-shirts theatrically mix drinks, tossing bottles in the air and catching them behind their backs and pouring the liquor with a flourish. Low tables surrounded by plush seats claim space throughout the bar; they are coveted by the drinkers who came too late and now have to stand in sweaty, awkward groups.

Cora told her husband that she had to go to a work function this evening. It was something she couldn't avoid, she'd said. Necessary for her career, important clients, it will be dull, but must be endured. Sacrifices must be made. It's not that she needed to lie, her husband wasn't the controlling type but he never went out with friends any more, his whole life revolved around her and the children, so she felt that admitting she needed any life outside of the family would be sacrilegious, an affront at the very least to his company and the world they had constructed behind the blue door of their house. She was defecting, looking elsewhere, happier outside the sanctuary he'd created for them all. A sanctuary built of red brick, pitch pine and slate tile, Farrow and Ball paints and real wool rugs.

She imagined he would be watching TV, his feet propped up on the coffee table in front of the sofa. He would be perfectly happy, self-contained, the kids sleeping in their rooms. Everything would be in order. Just right. Without her there, toxic and suppurating like a flesh-eating lesion. She lies in order to do good. Breaking her mother's rules just to keep afloat.

A man in a black t-shirt with the bar's logo across his chest steps into their huddle and puts down a tray loaded with shot glasses of Jagermeister.

'Wayheyhey!' Sonja shouts. The others laugh and reach for a glass. Sonja hands one to Cora, grinning.

'On three! Ready? One, two, three.' The women down the shots, tipping their heads back and draining the glasses before slamming them down on the table, their faces gurning and grimacing. Cora swallows hers down and feels the comforting heat trace a hot line through her body. Her pulse beats in time to the music. The other women are shouting jokes and quips at each other over the music. Nudging each other when a man they like the look of walks past.

'Let's get more,' Cora says and the others laugh and shout yes. They call over the barman who takes their order and then returns with more shots. They knock them back. The evening is progressing well. Cora sluices the sticky Jagermeister from her teeth and tongue with a swig from her glass of wine, its metallic taste neutralizing the sugary booze. Her head swims and her eyes feel heavy. She is fleshy and hot, sticky with sweat. She laughs along with the others, not totally sure of what she is laughing at, but she joins in, she knows the drill. It feels good to know the ropes for once, to know what is expected of her and how to play along. Her face aches from pulling unfamiliar expressions, her muscles contract and release as she mimics the others, but it's OK. It's working. She fits in perfectly.

Cora leans over to Sonja and shouts, 'I'm just going to the ladies.' Sonja nods. Cora stands, drunk but still steady on her feet. She tucks her bag under her arm and totters through the bar, navigating around the groups of drinkers. She is unseen, like the wild animals that share the city, there but not there. She is too old to be visible in here. Over the hill, past it. No longer viable. She pushes through, shouldering into bodies that block her way. They may not see her but they will feel her. She is angry. It's as if she is covered by a layer of anger, like a layer of subcutaneous fat. Always present, ready to rage. She reaches the toilet and blinks in the bright light before almost falling into a cubicle. She locks the door and hitches her skirt up over her hips before sitting heavily on the toilet.

She pisses, her belly emptying. She sighs with relief, her knickers around her knees. The cubicle is clean, with minimal graffiti; she supposes only adults use these toilets. Accordingly, there are stickers offering the numbers of counselling services and taxi firms. A poster reminds her that the police will protect her if her partner is abusive; the poster also conveniently lists the types of abuse one might encounter. She wipes herself, stands and pulls up her knickers, smoothing her skirt down. She washes her hands, avoiding her reflection. She doesn't want to think about her husband or children, but they prey on her mind constantly, no matter what, she can't shake loose. She is an animal in a trap that will have to resort to chewing off its own limb to escape.

She can hear someone in the other cubicle, sniffing and snorting at something. Cora wonders whether, if she hangs around, maybe the occupant of the cubicle would share whatever she is snorting. She would like to try it, whatever it is. She would like to numb her brain, interrupt its faculties, stick a spanner in the works. But she is scared, a wimp, a coward. She has never got high. She doesn't wait and leaves the room, pushing at the door so hard so that it swings out and hits the wall behind with a loud bang.

As she walks back through the bar a man steps in her way.

'Hello. I know you, don't I?' He is tall and thin, with reddish blond hair cut short over his ears. His thin lips pull back in a smile revealing perfect teeth.

'I don't think so.' Cora steps back a little, manoeuvring air and space between them.

'Yes, I do. You work with Dave, don't you? Dave MacAdam.' He takes a drink from his bottle of beer and smiles. He is very smiley. Cora can smell his cologne, a lemony scent mixed with the smell of cigarettes and beer.

'Yes, that's right. I don't remember you though.'

'Well, that's probably because I'm a consultant, in and out depending on the whims of your boss. My name's Chris, by the way.'

'Oh right. Now I'm embarrassed. Of course I remember you.'

'No, no that's alright. I'm not very memorable.' He shrugs his shoulders and tilts his head to one side, looking at her sideways as if trying to be coquettish. Cora swallows, coughs and shifts her balance, getting ready to move on.

'Drink?' Chris nods towards the bar, 'What can I get you?'

'Erm. Sure,' she says and reaches her hand to her neck before dropping it again to her side. 'A vodka and tonic, please.'

'OK.' He winks at her and turns to the bar to order their drinks.

Cora looks around the room. It is crammed with people, drunk, horny people, half visible in the low blue light. Most of them are touching in some way: holding hands, groping buttocks or breasts, kissing, grinding. It's getting late. The women she was with are talking to a group of men. They look relaxed, happy. She is a slut who shouldn't be here. But this is the best place for her, a meat market for available flesh. She doesn't deserve her lovely, well-ordered home or her husband but most especially she doesn't deserve her children.

Chris nudges her and hands her a drink. He holds out his beer and clinks it against her glass.

'Cheers!'

'Yes, cheers.' She drinks, ice knocking against her teeth.

'You know, you have a very sexy walk.' Chris stands close to her, too close; anyone looking at them would think they were lovers.

'No, I didn't know that.'

'Well you do. A very sexy walk.' He takes her hand and strokes the tips of her fingers with his. She lets him. He is an expert at seduction. She won't resist. He moves closer and strokes the palm of her hand and then grasps it in his. Looking at her, watching her. She twists his wedding ring around his finger.

'Is that a problem?' he asks.

The loud music pounds at Cora's head. She can't think straight. 'Do you want to come outside?' She says. 'It's so loud in here.'

'Yes, sure.'

They walk together through the bar, past her friends who don't notice her leaving. Chris's hand is on the small of her back, guiding her around the small crowds of people like he is steering a small vessel or an imbecile. They step outside into the quiet, cool street. Orange light fills the space, expanding from the streetlight above, its electric hum accompanying the click of her heels. They walk together past the small crowd of smokers out on the pavement, his arm around her now, possessive, claiming her. It feels good. She disgusts herself and is surprised by how comforting that is. Taxis trundle past, their lights glowing.

'This road is usually so busy, full of traffic. S'weird to see it so quiet.'

'I know. Like an alternate reality.' Cora moves faster now. She leads him past the empty offices and closed shops. She turns off Bishopsgate into a side street, towards the shelter of a doorway. She turns and leans against the wooden door. A fire escape.

'You know your way around,' he says. She says nothing, just looks at him, her face blank, unreadable in the dark.

He steps in close and strokes her. His moves follow the usual order: first kissing, then stroking breasts, moving down the body towards her bottom and then trying to lift the skirt. She's seen it all before. It's a ritual, a dull routine. ABC. Meanwhile she is expected to return kisses, arch her back and moan, all while rubbing and stroking his penis. None of this will do for what Cora needs. What Cora must have. Now.

She sinks to the ground, grit and cigarette butts pressing into her knees. She unzips his trousers, looking up at him. He is staring down at her, his mouth hanging open. He can't believe his luck. She takes his cock in her mouth and holding him by the hips she pulls him deep into her throat. She is ravenous. He groans and lets his head drop onto his chest. His eyes closed, he rocks his hips back and forth.

'Mmmm, you are not what I expected. Oh God. Oh God. You are something else.'

He rests his hands on her head and strokes her hair. He is sharing a gentle, consensual encounter with her. But she requires something else. She stands and faces the wall, pulling up her skirt and tugging her knickers over to one side.

'Fuck me hard. Now.'

He pushes himself into her, grunting, holding her hips. She barely feels a thing. She is female, she is receptive, well-practiced. He slides in and out. She can hear him, grunting and breathing over her shoulder. She pushes back against him. There is a freedom in fucking a stranger: you can be yourself, uninhibited. You can demand that they service your needs because you will never have to see them again, knowing that they've seen the sickest part of you.

'Please,' she says, 'Do it harder.' He responds, banging harder against her body, pushing her up against the wall.

'Harder,' she demands. 'Harder. Pull my hair.'

He pauses for a moment and then does as she asks, but carefully, restrained. He takes a handful of her hair and tugs it, playful. Acting.

'You're kinky. I like it, baby.'

Her need overwhelms her, pours out of her like fluid spewing up and out, hot and vengeful. She wants revenge against herself. She wants to feel his fist in her cunt, in her face, in her arse. She wants him to kick her in the guts. She begs him: 'Hurt me. Please. Hit me. Punch me.' She thinks of her family, all cosy in their snug, clean beds. 'Please Chris. Hit me.'

'I'm not that kind of man, baby. Let me make you come.' He reaches around to touch her clit, and rubs at her, confident he can make her feel good. 'Is that good, Cora? Is that good?' He keeps thrusting and rubbing, his breathing coming in hot spurts. 'I'm close, I'm really close. Come with me. Come with me.'

Cora pulls away and drops to her knees again.

'Oh yeah,' Chris moans. 'Let me come in your mouth.'

Cora puts his cock back in her mouth and bites down on the smooth skin. She bites hard. Chris screams and shoves her away from him. 'What the fuck is wrong with you?' He checks himself to see if she has drawn blood. 'Jesus fucking Christ.'

'Hit me,' Cora says. 'I deserve it. Hit me back.' She stands up straight as he does up his trousers, watching her all the while. 'Come on, Chris, I'm a sick whore. Hit me back. Please.' She is breathless, almost dizzy.

He shakes his head, his eyes wide. 'You're fucking sick you are. You're mental. You need help. Jesus Christ.' He pushes her again and almost runs to the main road, looking back to check she isn't behind him. She watches him go, his taste in her mouth, before straightening her clothes and moving in the same direction towards the street. She looks up and down the road. There's no trace of him, he has gone. Only a small group of smokers stand out on the pavement. Cora wipes her mouth on the back of her hand and hails a black cab. Something must be done.

*I remember you marching towards me, head to toe in black.
Black leather boots, black long coat, black scarf wrapped around
your neck, black hat. Your cigarette held like a weapon, stabbing
at the air, your arm swinging forwards and back. I thought to
myself, she's like an entire regiment in one person coming towards
me. You were surefooted, even in the deep snow. I was waiting
for you, my breath coming in smoky gusts, leaning against the
station entrance. We were going to a New Year's Eve party in
York. We were taking the train so we could both relax, snooze
and read the papers all the way there. I'd brought along a bottle
of red wine and some plastic cups: at the time I thought it was
a romantic gesture.*

*It seemed as if the entire world was weighed down by light. And
silence. The snow revealing something terrible. Something usually
hidden in the dirt and the bustle of the ordinary. Sometimes it is
best to remain in the dark. Not knowing. What you don't know
can't hurt you. Isn't that what they say? Cora?*

*We took a taxi to our friends' place and they showed us to
our room at the top of the house. A neat, plain spare room. You
said it was a good room. A pale striped counterpane covered
the double bed, a small jug of water and two glasses were on
the side table, next to a small pile of National Geographic
magazines. You pointed to them and raised an eyebrow 'What
a good hostess!' and slumped down onto the bed. You stretched
and arched your back. I came over and, leaning on my knuckles,
kissed you. You laughed and whispered 'not now, they're waiting
for us', even as you locked your legs around my waist and pressed
your warm body against mine. Then you rolled out from under
me, laughing, teasing, brushing against my erection, and went to
stand at the window.*

*The window looked out onto their back garden, and their
neighbours' gardens. Long rectangles of grass and paving, ponds*

and bird tables, rickety sheds, BBQs and lawn furniture lay forgotten under the snow. Everything was forgotten, concealed, by my aching need for you at that moment. But you'd gone, standing there in front of me, I could see you'd drifted away into thoughts that excluded me, as if I were concealed by the snow.

In the kitchen, you helped with the food. You'd changed into a red dress with thin straps, even in high heels it skimmed the floor, a red full-length column. You weren't wearing a bra, I noticed. You wore your engagement ring and the gold stud earrings I'd bought you for Valentine's Day. I watched you arrange hunks of cheese and bunches of grapes on a board with piles of biscuits. You chatted easily with Josie, the hostess, the wife of an old school friend of mine, as she cut up carrots and cucumber into fingers. You'd always liked her. You said she wasn't ordinary, she wasn't a walking cliché. You'd darkened your eyes with make-up but your cheeks were pink from the heat and your glass of wine. You were gorgeous. At some point you looked up and saw me watching and called me over to help: you said something like 'stop gawping and start chopping' and I came over and stood next to you, your perfume filling my head as I clumsily tried to slice the vegetables. I was intoxicated by you, by the way you laughed and shook your hair back from your shoulders. By the way you bit into a tomato without spoiling your lipstick, the points of bone at the base of your throat.

You danced all night long. Sometimes with me, sometimes alone. You smiled to yourself, sipping from your glass of champagne. The house was crowded with guests; moving from the kitchen to the sitting room to the dining room was a challenge. People stood on the stairs, shouting and laughing over the music. I lost sight of you at one point and thought nothing of it, stood chatting and laughing with Matt, my old friend, Josie's husband. Then I saw you again, this time leaning against the kitchen window, looking out, one hand pressed against the glass, one hand holding a cigarette, smoking, watching the fireworks from another party in the street. The red dress falling around your body. You've not

153

worn it since. You say it no longer fits, that the children put paid to all that. It is in the dressing up trunk in Jessica's bedroom, my grandfather's old steamer truck stamped with his initials and now containing a profusion of different people for the children to try on: a soldier, a nurse, a princess, a pirate, a red Indian and a younger, happier version of you.

I grabbed you at one point and, drunk, slid my hand inside your dress, my fingers grazing a nipple. You leaned closer to me and kissed me with an open mouth. Then you were dancing again, whirling around in flashes of red. The rented disco lights pulsed against the pushed-back furniture and clumsy dancing bodies; empty glasses collected on the mantelpiece and plates of half-eaten food were piled on the bookshelves. The forgotten Christmas tree wilted in the corner. I watched you, my fingertips still warm from your breast. I needed a drink and pushed through to the kitchen and past Josie and Matt arguing in the corner, trying not to be heard. Always the perfect hosts. I pulled another bottle of champagne from the fridge; they didn't notice me. You smiled as I filled your glass, I didn't mention the argument being hissed out in the other room. I knew you'd say it was none of our business.

Then the music was switched off and the TV switched on. Everyone piled into the room; Josie appeared and handed out party poppers and streamers, smiling. Matt stood in the doorway watching. The countdown began and we all joined in and shouted ten, nine, eight, seven, six... You squeezed my hand and kissed me and I cupped your face and said 'Happy New Year, my darling.' We were excited like small children, like we still believed in a magical renewal, that the new year promised something special for us. Then we were swept up and moved on by the crowd of shouting and laughing friends. Grabbed from behind, I turned to find Matt and hugged him. You clutching your glass, as you smiled and kissed and hugged everyone that you passed. Streamers and party poppers exploded, someone lit sparklers.

Other people separated us, but I could see you, on the other side of the room, smiling and enjoying yourself.

He kissed you, there in the crowded room. Everyone was kissing, calling 'Happy New Year!' as the chimes of Big Ben sounded out from the TV, everyone shaking hands, hugging, I kissed Josie and others, of course. I saw him kiss you again, his hand in the small of your back, holding you to him, the full length of your body pressed against his, your lovely breasts warm against his chest, I saw the tip of your tongue push forward into his mouth. You kissed him, really kissed him and then you pulled away and laughed. Josie saw it too. I looked over at her and she was watching you both.

We woke late of course, with hangovers, and went downstairs to find Josie already up and throwing paper plates of food into a black plastic sack. Matt was still in bed. You kissed her on the cheek and made coffee. He didn't wake while we put the house back in order. Slept through the rattle of empty bottles being piled up outside the front door. Josie made bacon sandwiches for us all and we sat quietly in the kitchen, too tired, too hungover to talk much. You smoked a cigarette. We'd already packed our bag. The red dress was folded away with your high-heeled sandals and my shirt and tie. We left, Josie seeing us off from her front door and we walked to the train station in the cold. The pavement was still icy and you held my arm as we walked. You said, 'How odd that Josie didn't wake Matt up to at least say goodbye...' and I nodded and said nothing. What you don't know can't hurt you.

The chairs in the waiting room are surprisingly comfortable. Cora sits in the corner, unobtrusive, but as she is the only client there she can't hide. The receptionist let her in with a smile. Her voice was immediately recognisable from their phone conversation the day before. The consulting rooms are housed in a converted flat. She climbed three flights of stairs to the top of the building before knocking on the door. The waiting room is small with a black leather sofa and several straight-backed chairs. There are no plants, and blinds at the window are drawn against the daylight, but a pile of magazines is neatly placed on a coffee table. Classical music plays in the background. The receptionist sits behind a cheap black-ash desk, answering the telephone and shuffling papers. When Cora arrived, the receptionist handed her a questionnaire on a clipboard with a biro. Diligently she answers every question. She has come for help after all.

A bell rings and the receptionist looks up at Cora. 'She's ready to see you now. If you go through that door and into the room opposite, she'll meet you there. OK?'

Cora stands and places the clipboard on the chair before stepping towards the door.

'You need to take the questionnaire.' The receptionist is absolutely professional: everything must be done correctly. Cora stops, turns and apologises, her cheeks flush, she picks up the clipboard and hurries out of the room. Nerves unbuckle her limbs, she almost falls over, her knees give way. Cora leans back against the white wall, sweat lines her brow, her hair clings to her face as if she has just emerged from a plunge underwater. She breathes to steady herself, pulls her bag over her shoulder and tucks the clipboard under her arm. She must take the next step. She knocks on the door and enters.

The room is tiny and painted magnolia. A framed picture of a woman in high heels decorates one wall. Another door in the opposite wall is shut but represents another space.

'Come in, hi, I'm Joyce. Take a seat.' The woman sits on a sofa, her legs crossed. She is wearing a plain black dress revealing her cleavage and shiny stiletto shoes. She is plump, her arms and legs rounded with good meat. Her face is lacquered with make-up, but discreetly: she wears only a little eye shadow and lip-gloss, nothing too obvious, nothing that could scare Cora away. Her hair is red and curly and bounces loose around her shoulders. Cora sits on the sofa, pressed against the arm, as far away from the woman as is polite.

She found the number easily enough. Typed in the key words on the Internet. She wasn't particularly discerning, picking the first one she found in the area. Not too near, not too far. With parking. There was no mention of prices on the website or the exact address, but the receptionist had given all the information over the phone including recommending a gift of £150.00, cash only. Cora wondered if that meant the price was negotiable but didn't dare ask. She went to the bank on her way there and took the money from the joint savings account. Before he notices it has gone she'll find a way to replace it. He won't check it. Not for months. He can't see what's under his nose. It's essential she gets treatment: she is sick and must be cured.

'Some of my clients think of me as their therapist. It's not what most people imagine here. You're entirely safe and secure. Think of it as your private space.' Joyce takes the clipboard from Cora and reads it through quickly. Well practiced, she can glean the information she needs in seconds, like a doctor examining the shadows of an x-ray. Symptoms and the cure required are instantly revealed to the professional. Cora sits pressing her knees together, crisply outlined in her summer dress. Her muscles are tensed; her palms are damp. She half expects the woman to reach forward and press the glands in her neck, palpating under the jaw for abnormalities. Cora respects

157

doctors, dentists, teachers: experts of any kind. She will gladly entrust herself to their capable attentions. They know better than she does.

'So. Tell me why you've come to see me.' The woman's voice is deep, almost masculine.

'I want to be punished. I can't do it myself. I want the pain I've caused others. I want to suffer.'

'That's not a problem. Do you have any idea how you'd like this pain administered?'

'No. Not really. I want you to hurt me.'

'Well, we have the usual whips and floggers. We have electrics here that give small controlled shocks; we have a suspension rack, a bondage table. There's nipple torture for example. There's suturing, I can sew up your vagina, or pierce your skin with surgical needles.'

Cora begins to liquefy like wax; she is malleable, half solid, half liquid. 'I really don't know. You decide.'

'OK. For instance, would you like humiliation along with punishment? I mean name calling, etc. that kind of thing.'

'No, don't speak. I just want to feel my body again. Just physical.'

'Right, well. Can you be marked?'

Cora nods. What difference does any of it make now? None of this matters. She has slipped through the cracks. She must make amends. She has entered another universe, hygienically sealed off, quarantined. What you don't know can't hurt you. The outside world continues buying and selling, loving and hating. Moving forwards, in a straight line, one-way traffic.

'Well, it takes practice. I've had clients who've been coming for years, and it takes time to be able to take the deeper SM work. I've been training some slaves for a very long time.' Cora opens her mouth to speak. 'I realise you aren't a slave. Trust me, I've seen all sorts. We'll begin slowly. Any questions?'

'I don't think so. You understand I want to suffer. I want you to punish me because I'm too cowardly to do it myself. I don't want a game. I don't want you to dress up or talk like the people in those films.' Cora is exhilarated by her own honesty. Her skin constricts in tight goose pimples, the hairs on the back of her neck stand up. Her flesh responds to her voice.

'Are you sure you don't want me to wear something to heighten the experience? Most people do you know.' Joyce sits forward, tapping her fingers on the clipboard.

'No. Just as you are, please. I don't want dressing up. I'm not a child. I don't want to play. Please.'

Joyce sits back, watching Cora, assessing her. 'OK. If you step in there,' Joyce points to the closed door on their right. 'Get undressed, evacuate your bladder and bowels if you can and wait to be summoned. You can leave your things on the stool in there. Please leave your gift for me in the envelope provided. We have thirty minutes left.'

Cora opens the door and steps into the bathroom. A small mirror hangs above the sink. A shower cubicle takes up most of the space, surrounded by a glass barrier. She undresses, placing her clothes on the stool provided. She leaves the money in the envelope and squats on the toilet bowl as instructed. Shame conceals her nakedness. She washes her hands, feeling nothing: the acid of hatred has burnt away her nerve endings. In the mirror she sees the features of herself. Recognising the face, the hair, the neck. She is a composition, a collection of features that mark her out. She pictures the children, their demanding, clutching limbs, their hungry faces, their toes and fingers, grasping, grasping. Natural demands that ask too much of her. She is defined by what she is unable to give. She is defined by her lack. She is lack, a void, a blank space that devours. Takes, takes, takes. She cannot give.

The door opens. 'On your knees and follow me.' Cora follows Joyce, crawling on her hands and knees through the room and down the corridor. Her blood flows, carrying oxygen to her organs, her brain. Tied by blood to the children, it's in the blood, the poisoned code. The rough carpet needles against her hands and knees. Suspended on its fibres, held apart from the ground beneath her. Joyce opens the door ahead of them and waits for Cora. 'Hurry up.' Already the experience has become a farce. The room is large and clean. The walls are padded and covered in bright red rubber sheeting. Black rubber- and leather-covered tables and benches furnish the room. It is dark, lit only by a couple of small lamps. Cora doesn't know the names of the items she can see. She is without the language necessary to belong. She is only flesh. Shelves line one wall, and under these whips and canes hang from hooks like drying carcasses. A metal frame with ropes and pulleys stands in the centre of the room. There is nothing original present. Everything is as one would expect. Like a cartoon. People demand absolute knowledge, which can only lead to cliché. Like duty and exhausted expectations from which one can only ever fail.

'We'll warm you up first.' Already there is too much talking. Cora's mouth fills with saliva. She swallows it back. Once she was a girl capable of feeling intensely. Now she is alive only to hatred. She has anaesthetised herself. She must be pulled back. 'Lean over the pommel horse there, now.' Joyce points to a humped four-legged piece, an imitation of gym equipment. She leans over it, the smooth covering of leather pressed delicately against her skin, animal to animal. Joyce bends down, pulling on Cora's wrists and buckling her to the legs of the furniture, spread armed, then spread legged over the decapitated thing. Cora can smell the counterfeit peach perfume of Joyce's shampoo. Exposed, she is in direct contact with the air. She breathes in herself, molecules that have clung to her own skin and hair, she breathes them in and then out. Exposed to herself. She does not resist, lies slack over the pommel, held tight by the ligatures that tie off the poison. She is a host, a community of bacteria and parasites. She closes her eyes, blinding her self.

Behind her she can hear the other woman moving around the room, lifting objects, putting things back. She is content to stay in the luxury of this bondage. Unable to move, she is waiting.

She is a machine that produces unsatisfactory merchandise. She is ready to be fixed. The footsteps move towards her and further away from her. She is the centre of the room. The reason for its being. She must service the room as it must service her. Together they exist. The room and her. She is only what the room will make of her. Done up as it as in cheap theatricals, a set designed to showcase her suffering. It doesn't matter. Only that she is forced back into shape, that repentance will bring change. That her materials are altered irrevocably. She demands that she is transformed by suffering.

The room is hot, but columns of cooler air are pumped from the ceiling. Blood runs to her head, pooling in the cup of her skull. Discomfort begins to spread through her body. Love comes packaged in violence. A split second is marked by the sharp crack of a whip. Her buttocks tense, the muscles contract, electrical pulses signal the nerve endings. Cora exhales. Her hands and feet are numb. She sees only black. Her body sags against the support of the horse. Another second is counted out, crack, then another and another. She gasps, that counts out two seconds. She has access to the purity of physical time. Time played out in sensation and movement. Time that transcends the play of light. Joyce changes tack. Changes the weapon that will deliver the passion to Cora.

Cora feels the split straps of the flogger curling around her thighs as they impact. She is forced back into herself. She is entirely alone inside her body, isolated, held apart. The sensation lingers and vibrates, remaining to greet the next impact. Joyce changes tack again: this time the sting of a riding crop flicks against her thighs, as fleeting as a dizzy spell on rising from a chair; time is defined by sensation. The split pulse of a slap: quavers, crochets, semibreves. Together she and Joyce battle with her degradation. She is unworthy of Joyce's attention. She hangs there in contemplation, approaching sanctification. It continues, time beaten out. Repeats. She silences herself; she must endure without a sound. Annulled, she is nothing more than a being capable of sensation; she's an animal at last. No thoughts, no longing for a belief system in which she could deposit her anguish. Stripped bare she is immersed in a private pool of mortification, a series of perfect pains. She pays for the failure of her flesh, for the promiscuity of molecules that gave birth to the children.

Cora is lost in the rapture of forgetting, of returning to her body, entirely feeling. She is bestial. A live thing: alive. Crawling; breathing; eating; defecating. She feasts on the intimacy of being beaten. Of being recognised. A dung beetle collecting shit. Joyce mothers her, castigates and loves. Love is labouring to improve our defective loved ones. Love takes as its responsibility the need to chastise and remould. Love takes a half-formed thing and remakes it into something worth having around. Alive, living fully, her blood rushing through her, she exhausts her self. Panting like a dog, drool drips from the corner of Cora's mouth onto the floor. She has marked the room. Her thighs and buttocks burn. She wants more. Forces the word from her animal mouth, twisting her tongue around the sound. 'More. More.' Behind her the arm raises and falls, beating out the seconds and minutes. There are no hours left.

'Harder.' It can never be hard enough. 'More.'

'Time's up I'm afraid.'

'More.' Cora shakes her head, trying to see Joyce as she moves about the room re-hanging the implements she used, after wiping them with antiseptic. She turns the lights up. The room is revealed. Truth penetrates the dark, unveiling the farce, the ludicrous nature of Cora's self-delusion. Joyce kneels in front of her. Unbuckling the restraints around her wrists and ankles.

'You did really well! I thought we'd have to stop or at least move you around. Well done!'

Cora's body is heavy, outraged. She is numb. She is an illusion.

'Up you get. Slowly, though. OK. When you're ready. I've got another one booked in so we need to get the room tidied and cleaned.' Cora attempts to stand. Her head fuddled by too much blood. She is limp with knowledge. Disembodied. The pain failed to eradicate her hatred. She pulls herself up and leans on the pommel. It continues to support her. Her skin is raw. She reaches her fingertips to her buttocks. She can trace the elegant welts that identify her. She has been written on.

'Right then, let's get you into the changing room.' This excess of words, of a tried and tested language harries at Cora. She feels sick. Standing on an unsteady floor, she rocks back and forth. Movement forwards on her feet is beyond her. Staying absolutely still, rooted to the spot is her only possibility of redemption. An excess of growth, limbs could become boughs, become leaves; unmoving, tree-like she could cling to the ground and be saved. Moving now, she can go in only one direction. She must leave the room, get dressed, leave the building and be at liberty, on the loose. She must move. There is no choice. She can only move forwards.

In the bathroom she dabs at her new wounds. They smart and twitch as she presses them; thin lines of watery blood stain the tissue. She pulls her underwear on over her cuts and dresses herself. She is neither possessed by the wounds nor does she possess them. She is unmoved. Unchanged. Except she now has this encounter to add to her original shame. She has suffered but it makes no difference whatsoever. She continues to recede; her animal shape is reclaimed by her human stupidity, her cruelty and desires.

The receptionist waits for Cora in the corridor. She is to be ushered out to protect both her and the new customer's privacy. There must be no crossover, no mistaken recognition of a fellow penitent. They must remain anonymous. The girl smiles, a token of harmlessness, her blue eyes thickly rimmed with black make-up. She moves past Cora back into the bathroom. She discreetly, but still within full sight, pockets the envelope, checking first that it contains the requisite amount of money. Satisfied, she smiles again at Cora and pushes her hair from her face. She has small hands. Tiny hands like a child, almost deformed, but not quite: they are perfectly formed, just out of proportion as if the growth of her hands were stunted by a genetic abnormality. She notices Cora staring and tucks her midget hands behind her back.

'Is everything OK? Do you need anything before you go?' Cora shakes her head. There is nothing more they can do for her. Nothing penetrates the thick hide covering her rage. 'Would you like to book in your next appointment? Mistress Joyce will give you a ten percent discount if you book five appointments in advance.'

'No, thank you.' Cora moves forwards, only forwards. She has no other choice. The paint on the front door is chipped. Everything is disintegrating. Forwards through the door. The door is shut behind her. She will not go back there. She stands on the landing loitering for one moment. The bright blue of the summer sky is suspended in the window frame ahead of her.

I don't know you anymore. Can you ever really know someone? Can you ever really even know yourself? With everything in constant flux, nothing and no one stays the same. I understand this and I understand that relationships can't remain static. I know that our needs change, but I imagined that we would change and grow together, that we would talk about these things, I didn't imagine you would just go and have an affair. I know there is someone else. There are signs. I can read you like a book. You are so distant and snappy with me. You aren't where you say you will be, I call you at work and you're not there, they say you've taken the day off sick, but you aren't at home. What the hell else can that mean? When you get dressed for bed, you turn away from me so I can't see your body. You won't have sex with me and when we do, it's like you're thinking about someone else. You hardly look at me. I know there is someone else, I know. You're smoking again. I smell it on you and you gave up for me, for the kids, all that time ago. It's another betrayal, another promise you've broken. Maybe that's what you do with him. You have sex and you smoke post-coital cigarettes together. You have long lunches together and then fuck in a hotel, or his flat, perhaps he's not married. Maybe you make plans together about leaving and setting up a new life. I'm sure you've told him all about our children, he probably imagines he could be their new dad, I imagine he looks at the photos of them in your purse and thinks to himself how charming they are and how he could love them. Who the fuck does he think he is? The bastard. What does he look like, I wonder? How did you meet him? Where? When? Endless questions that are driving me mad. But the kids can't suffer because of this. It will be the children that are victims in all this and I won't allow that. They must be protected at all cost. It's my fault. I've not paid enough attention to you and now you've met someone else. It's my fault. I understand. Perhaps I should've done more for you; perhaps I've missed the early warning signs. Actually, I don't understand, it's not my fault. I've tried, I try every day.

I think about you, and I think about me and the worst thought I have is that we, as we know ourselves, as we think about ourselves and each other, my worst imagining is that we don't really exist, that all we are is mimics, that all us humans somehow just mimic behaviour, like a million parrots, a million mynah birds, pretending to speak and pretending to mean something. Meaning nothing. There is nothing original in all this. That is my worst thought. That none of this is real. That what we call love is just a pattern of behaviours that we've picked up along the way. I can't bear the idea that these feelings I have for you all are just something I've learnt to imagine. That we are only ever reproductions of a set of expectations. Anything else, we can survive. I need to know we are real, that these feelings are mine and mine alone. I will get over it. It's only sex, and good marriages weather the storm. People have affairs. They do, they have them and they survive and their marriage is all the stronger for it. This is a good marriage. It is. And I won't let you take the kids. I won't. I'm a good man and a good dad. You're a good mother. You will not leave me. I won't let you go, because I know you love the children so very much that you will take them with you and I can't allow that. I won't be a weekend father, gradually becoming a stranger to our children. Hanging around parks and pizza restaurants in the few hours you and the court would grant me with them, ashamed to take them back to my flat. I know the story; I've seen it happen to my friends. It won't happen that way for us.

The kids have woken up. They've switched the TV on in the sitting room. Are you really asleep I wonder? Or are you lying there waiting for me to go so that you can be alone with thoughts of him. What does it matter? We will talk; you and I, *and we will fix this. We were made for each other and we'll be happy again. I'll go down, make tea and clean the kitchen. Get everything ready. I want to make you happy, Cora. That's all.*

A shock of birds flies past the window, interrupting the blue with the brown flicker of wings. Cora turns her palms inwards to hide her lies. Standing at the top of the stairs. The truth exceeds the facts. She is mad with the desire for grace. She can only move forwards. Her body intervenes in the space between herself and the outside world. She can't move without there being a consequence that is unacceptable to her. Thoughts resembling the birds outside dart about her head. She breathes, in and out. Repeat. Repeat. Repeat. The house: the children: the car: the husband: her parents. She forgets them. Like birds the thoughts escape their cage. They fly away. They never existed. She forgets.

Forgetting takes no time at all. She looks down at her hands. They are clean. She leaves, moves down the stairs, into the street. She walks to her car. She reaches down and removes her shoes, placing them neatly together. Next to them she places her bag. She moves forwards, there is only forwards. She is only human and has no capacity for moving in any other direction. She places one foot in front of the other, toe to heel, heel to toe. Pigeon steps. She has forgotten that winter will come. She feels however, with absolute certainty, the direction of the metallic currents of the Earth's magnetic fields. She is bound by its unyielding rules. Its flow.

Barefoot, she moves forwards. At the kerb, she stands still. Looking up at the blue space, she has a new vision, a new sight that is freed from habits and history. All around her it is business as usual. People, traffic, a dog, cats, birds. Sounds penetrate her new wounds. Everything continues as before. It repeats with the occasional minor variation. The Earth alters in minute side steps. No one will notice. Why should they? She is innocent, has made no impression on the world that will not be forgotten almost immediately. It is the most she can hope for.

Lifting her arms up as if she is about to leap or take flight, she steps forward, unthinking like an animal; she trusts only the immutable laws of physics. She is bound by the holiness of gravity, the second law of force. Faithful, hoping for grace; stepping only forwards, her feet bold beyond the edge of the kerb. She can't turn back; there is no opportunity for erasing what has been. As she walks out, she experiences nothing but sensation. She is nothing but flesh: sensate, animal, alive.

Acknowledgements

I owe an enormous debt of gratitude to those who have encouraged, critiqued, read, read and read again, listened, told me to shut up and get on with it and most importantly, those who believed I could. My amazing teachers, lecturers and mentor: Mrs Joan Howard, Mr. Bell, Prof Russell Celyn Jones, Will Self, Blake Morrison and Prof Simon Morgan Wortham. My incredible friends and family: Joe, Boo, Indie and Raif. Pearl and Sid Lamb. Rose, Bess and Rufus. Michelle, Rebekah, Tara, Gwynnie, Rosie and Geraldine. Vikki. Adelle and Ben. Sara and Lindsay. Julia. My brilliant editor, Hetha and equally wonderful publisher, Kevin. And of course, the many, many writers I've read and learnt from, been inspired by and can only trail behind...